misfits inc.

no. 4

the kingfisher's tale

mark delaney

PEACHTREE

ATLANTA

For Gilda

My first kiss.
My first love.
My John Denver friend.
Twenty-seven years ago,
and I remember every moment.

A FREESTONE PUBLICATION

Published by
PEACHTREE PUBLISHERS LTD.
494 Armour Circle NE
Atlanta, Georgia 30324
www.peachtree-online.com

Text © 2000 by Mark Delaney

Background cover photo © DiMaggio/Kalish/The Stock Market
Inset cover photo © Kennan Ward/The Stock Market

Book and cover design by Loraine M. Balcsik
Composition by Melanie M. McMahon

Manufactured in the United States of America

10 9 8 7 6 5 4 3 2 1
First Edition

Library of Congress Cataloging-in-Publication Data

Delaney, Mark.
    The kingfisher's tale/Mark Delaney.—1st ed.
        p. cm.
        — (Misfits, Inc.; no. 4)
Summary: The discovery of dead birds in a national forest leads the four teenaged members of the Misfits, Inc. to investigate a mystery involving logging, militant environmental groups, congressional campaign contributions, and revenge.
        ISBN 1-56145-226-2
        [1. Environmental protection—Fiction. 2. Mystery and detective stories.] I. Title. II. Series:
Delaney, Mark. Misfits, Inc. ; no. 4
PZ7.D373185 Ki 2000
[Fic] —dc21

00-008743

E-mail the author at: misfitsink@aol.com

table of contents

Acknowledgments

Special thanks to:

Renee Ittner-McManus,
Dear friend and fellow Monkee-Maniac.
South Carolina never had a better Lois Lane.

You kept Rebecca Kaidanov in line
and made sure she did what a real reporter would do.

prologue

Las Cruzas National Forest
Three years ago

Jerry Vitale worried about the kid. He hadn't yet recovered from the last few weeks. "Hey," he said, "how 'bout helping me over here?"

The kid threw a single, quick nod in Jerry's general direction, then walked toward him, chainsaw resting almost weightless on his right shoulder.

"Let's start with this one," Jerry said. "You take it. I'll…supervise."

Rolling up the sleeves of his flannel shirt past his forearms, Jerry gazed out over the work site. Most of the men, the old-timers especially, were working again with an air of carefree abandon, as though the last two weeks had never happened. Jerry nodded with approval. At least until the next battle, their work would continue without interruption, without negative publicity, without danger. The foolishness was over.

He gestured to the kid. *Go ahead.*

2   But the kid had not recovered as the old-timers had. The older lumberjacks had dealt with fanatical environmentalists—monkey-wrenchers—before. So when they had awakened about a week ago to discover the vandalism—fuel for the vehicles and the chainsaws stolen, gas lines in the heavy movers cut, fuel tanks contaminated with granulated sugar—they had been angry, but not surprised. A day later, when the papers broke the news of the vandalism, the work site teemed with anchormen from the evening news stations, protestors carrying placards and shouting through bullhorns, and some nut who lived atop a Scotch pine for three days until a judge ordered him down. Now the circus was over. Jerry had beaten them all through his quiet insistence that his company be allowed to harvest lumber when and where the law allowed. "Careful," said Jerry, "so it doesn't jump out of your hand when you start it."

The kid nodded and reached for the pull rope on the chainsaw.

The kid—Tim Breen was his name—was only nineteen and had joined Monarch Lumber a month or so ago. He was a little young for the job, Jerry knew, and completely lacking in experience, but physically he was a horse. The company always had a need for a strong back, and the old-timers like Eli wouldn't hold out forever. Best of all, Tim was easygoing, willing to learn, and eager to work hard. Even the veterans, as tough and wary as they were, would throw an arm across Tim's shoulder or smack him on the back when they told a joke. It was a warmth they didn't share with just anybody.

"Well—go on," said Jerry.

Tim gave the rope a firm tug, and the chainsaw roared to life.

"I hold it like this?" Tim hollered.

Jerry nodded. The kid knew how to handle a chainsaw—Jerry had certainly shown him enough times. It was just that after the monkey-wrenchers Tim had become a little skittish. Jerry knew he'd have to baby him for a couple more days.

He watched as Tim approached the tree and positioned the blade for the initial wedge cut. "Look what you're doing," Jerry shouted over the din. "If you cut there, what's the angle of the fall?"

The kid looked at him, then at the tree trunk, then at the space where, in a few minutes, the sixty-foot Douglas fir would strike the ground. In the path of its fall were two other trees. The fir could easily strike one, glance off it, and roll. Too unpredictable. Too dangerous.

Swallowing, Tim shifted a quarter turn around the trunk. "Maybe here would be better," he called.

Jerry nodded. "Maybe."

Tim once more laid the spinning chain against the base of the tree. It bit into the bark and sent up a fountain of sawdust. As the young man worked, Jerry watched, his calm presence seeming to give Tim a bit more confidence.

From behind him, Jerry heard a voice shouting his name. He turned to see Zachary Morgan, his partner at Monarch, striding toward him. Zach was gesturing at one of the trucks, his face a hard mask of anger. *Probably*

4 *another repair problem*, Jerry thought. *Leftover monkey-wrenching.* Sometimes it took a while to uncover all the damage.

Just as he turned to follow Zach, his ear caught an odd whine from the chainsaw. Jerry looked over his shoulder and saw the kid wrestling with the saw, his brow furrowed and his massive arms shuddering with the effort. The kid drew the saw back an inch or so, then pressed forward again. Jerry sensed the danger instantly. He raised his hand and shouted to Tim, but against the buzz of the chainsaw the young man could not hear him. Grimacing, Tim used all his strength to drive its blade into the soft wood.

Jerry heard a metallic *pwing*.

Like a striking snake, the rotating, bladed chain snapped and whipped out from the saw, lashing Tim across the neck and torso. The young man stumbled back a couple of steps, the saw dropping from his fingers and thudding against the forest floor. In the sudden silence, he gazed open-mouthed at the blood welling through the front of his torn shirt.

He stood, teetering like a cut tree before falling to the ground.

Jerry and Zach ran over to the kid. Jerry tore off Tim's shirt and examined the wound that ran from the kid's neck, across his chest, and along his stomach. Blood was everywhere; it was hard to see where all of it was coming from. Jerry pressed the kid's shirt as best he could against the wound, but there was too much damage, too much blood. Beneath him, the kid heaved and shook. Men came running over, stripping off their shirts for bandages. One of them grabbed the satellite phone and called for medical assistance.

Zach gazed at the tree. "Jerry…" he said. He pointed at the trunk where Tim had been cutting. Within the wood, glistening like the edge of a honed knife and made ragged by the saw's blade, was a length of steel.

Spiked! Monkey-wrenchers sometimes drove a steel spike into a tree to prevent the tree from being cut. The spike was invisible to loggers, and harmless to the tree, but deadly to a spinning chainsaw blade.

Jerry pressed harder on his makeshift bandage. The damage to Tim's neck was the worst. Jerry gave up trying to control the bleeding from the kid's chest, letting the others do what they could. Instead, he pressed the saturated shirt hard against the neck wound with both hands. The kid gazed up at him, his eyes wide and unfocused, his mouth opening and closing as though he were trying to form words.

"Don't talk," said Jerry.

The man holding the satellite phone waved his arm for Jerry's attention. "Medical team's on the way," he called.

An ambulance will never make it in time, thought Jerry.

Zach looked at him, as though overhearing the thought. "They won't send an ambulance through on the logging road," he said. "They'll send a chopper. He'll make it."

Jerry looked at the kid. Tim's eyes were blank and unseeing now. The young man tried once more to form

6 words, his mouth shaking in an odd, twisted pattern. Jerry shook his head. *No...no....*

Tim's body heaved once more. His eyes opened wide for a moment, stared deeply into Jerry's, then turned glassy. Jerry heard a deep breath escape from the kid, felt it brush the hairs of his forearm. Then Tim Breen's body relaxed completely, sagging to the ground.

"Come on," Jerry said between his clenched teeth. He gripped Tim's shoulders and gave them a gentle shake. "Come on!" He slapped Tim's cheek, but the eyes—the kid's eyes told him.

Too late.

Jerry continued to press the shirt into the wound. He looked at Zach, but his partner did not return the gaze. Instead, Zach stood quietly next to the spiked tree that had ended Tim's life. His hand reached out for one of the axes the men used to clear away smaller branches or to split logs for a fire. He gripped the ax with one hand and swung it around, allowing the blade to bite into the side of the tree.

As Jerry watched, Zach pulled the blade out and swung it again fiercely. His partner's motions seemed oddly machinelike. Again and again Zach yanked the blade from the tree and drove it in again, cleaving small chunks of wood with each swing, as though by hand, and by himself, he would tear the tree from the ground.

chapter
one

eugenia "Byte" Salzmann pedaled her bicycle up the steep incline. "Hurry! We're almost there," she shouted to her friends. The bike's soft, knobby tires bit into the trail, sending out a small fountain of dirt as Byte squeezed the brakes and skidded into a turn.

She looked over her shoulder and laughed. Her friends—Peter Braddock, Jake Armstrong, and Mattie Ramiro—clustered together on their own bikes perhaps thirty yards behind her, struggling. Each had risen off the seat of his bike and was leaning forward against the handlebars, bearing down against the slippery dirt. Byte wasn't even breathing hard.

She had to admit she had an unfair advantage on a dirt trail. Her bike was a Diamondback, a twenty-one-speed mountain climber that was geared so low Byte felt she could almost ride it up the side of a building. She took it now to the peak of the incline, hung there a moment, and cast another glance back at her friends. Then she shifted her weight forward and let the bike tilt into a final downward plunge. This was her favorite part of the ride. Here, the trail straightened, and she could feel herself picking up speed. The wind was cold against her face and made her eyes water. It tossed her hair and whistled through the vents of her riding helmet.

This part of the trail cut through several hundred acres of federally owned national forest. On either side of Byte were towering pine trees, thick with spring growth. Their needles glistened with moisture, dripping with the misty rain that had fallen only an hour ago.

Her destination was a clearing that lay just ahead. Byte squeezed the brakes and swung one leg over the silicone-filled seat, coasting the last few yards and jumping off as the bike slowed. Like many climbing bikes, hers was designed to be as lightweight as possible, so it had no kickstand. Byte leaned the bicycle against a tree and sat down in the clearing, slipping off her backpack and drawing in deep gulps of air. She tugged off her shoes and socks, digging her toes into the wet grass. Peter, Jake, and Mattie crested the hill, and Byte watched as their bikes bucked and shuddered beneath them, bouncing against the rocks and gouges in the trail.

"Hey," she said as the others pulled into the clearing, "we made it."

None of the guys said a word. Jake Armstrong swung off his bike and stamped down the kickstand with his foot. He sank onto the dirt, his back against a tree, his eyes closed, his face tilted up to the sky. Byte smiled. She

liked the way that Jake sometimes tuned out his sur-
roundings and turned his mind inward. Byte knew he
wasn't tired; Jake was the most athletic one in the group.
He was probably feeling the sun and the cool breeze,
drawing in the overpowering scent of pine in the air.
Maybe he was even turning those sensations into a day-
dream, or fashioning them into a line of music.

Peter Braddock looked around the clearing through
fogged glasses. Byte sensed he was mentally cataloguing
the sights, sounds, and smells of the area, filing them
away in that data disk of a brain. Two hours after they
left this place, Peter would no doubt be able to describe
every rock, insect, and plant within a twenty-foot
radius.

It was Mattie Ramiro who seemed to have the most
limited appreciation of the trip. Oblivious to the
scenery, he turned his attention to Byte's bike, fingering
the cables in the expensive Shimano derailleur system.
"Hey," he asked, "how does this work?" He tugged at one
of the shifters, and it clicked.

"Don't do that," Byte said.

Mattie shrugged, grinned, and sprawled out on the
grass.

These were Byte's friends. The four had met early in
high school, and Peter had named their group Misfits,
Inc.

"So," Jake finally said, "this is it, huh?"

Byte wrapped her arms around her knees and took in
a deep, satisfied breath. "Uh huh," she said. "This is it."

10 Peter leaned over and consulted the odometer on his bicycle. "We're exactly 4.7 miles from your mom's cabin," he noted. "What do you do here? I mean, it's a long way to ride just for the view."

Byte hesitated. Peter was so logical, so focused on precise detail. How could she make him understand that her love for this place was not based in logic, but emotion? Would Peter understand how, when she and her mom spent a weekend at their mountain cabin, Byte would cycle to this spot and rest against her special tree—the very one Jake was leaning against—until the sun began to fall? Could he comprehend the thrill she felt in summer when the clouds caught the sunset and streaked the sky above the dark trees with reds and oranges and purples? Or in winter when the pines were heavy with snow, and the wind blew the flakes off in thin, shimmering curtains? How could she make him understand that, in spring, a nearby stream swelled with meltwater, its quiet trickle becoming a gurgling rush, and that she found tremendous peace in that sound?

Byte often came here after difficult times at home or at school and rested, first crying, then laughing, then crying again until her insides felt clean.

"I just come here to think," she finally said. "To be alone."

Mattie plucked a strand of sourgrass from the dirt and stuck it in his mouth. "Cool," he said.

For several moments the four of them sat quietly, listening to the chatter of birds. Byte watched her friends, realizing that she had invited them out here specifically because she wanted to finally share this place with them. But one important part of the experience remained unexplored.

"Hey," she said quietly, slipping her shoes back on, "I want to show you guys something."

She rose, and the three boys followed her away from the path and deeper into the woods. She stepped through the grass and leafy plants that grew on the forest floor, leading them toward the sound of rushing water.

The stream was about twelve feet wide and probably a little over a foot deep. Its clear water bubbled over the stones that lined the bottom. Byte pointed here and there, showing the others some tiny fish swept along by the water's current. "Once all the snow melts," she said, "this stream will be half again as wide, and the water will come up to my knees." She squatted down and motioned to the others to do the same. "If we're really quiet," she whispered, "we might get to see something."

They waited silently for several minutes. Mattie, the youngest of the group, grew impatient and began tugging at a loose piece of bark on a tree. Byte scowled at him and shook her head. Next to her, Peter waited, looking at Byte with a raised eyebrow and a hint of a smile on his face. Byte figured he was enjoying the air of mystery she had created. Jake just shrugged and leaned toward a dandelion, blowing off its ball of cottony seeds.

12 Byte heard a birdcall and stared toward the upper branches of a tree. Something moved, and she pointed so the others could see it. "Look," she whispered.

In the tree was a large gray bird, about the size of an average pet-store parrot. It had a crest of bright red feathers along the top of its head, and a long, thin, needlelike beak that turned downward at the end. It sat up on its branch and called again.

Then it did something that delighted Byte and surprised the three boys. It dove down from the top of the tree, its wings half folded for speed, and shot toward the stream. Water splashed, wings fluttered, then the bird rose from the stream and glided back to its perch. Now a tiny fish squirmed in its beak. The bird made several jerking motions with its head and the fish slid down its gullet. The bird ruffled its feathers, spraying the water from them, and settled down again on the branch.

"That was amazing," whispered Jake.

"I looked up the bird in an Audubon field guide," said Byte. "It's a belted kingfisher. The females dig trenches next to streambeds and lay their eggs inside them." She looked at the others. "Come on," she said. "A little ways upstream, there's a small waterfall I want to show you."

She led them along the edge of the stream and up a small incline. The leafy plants tugged at their ankles and the moist earth was slippery, so they climbed by planting their feet against tree roots and small stones.

It was easy for Byte to lose herself in this place. Nature did for Byte what music did for Jake, what mastering a difficult sleight-of-hand magic trick did for Mattie, what a chess problem did for Peter. Even now as she watched, a gray squirrel chittered nearby, and Byte saw it scurry up a tree and out along a branch. As the branch thinned, it gave under the squirrel's weight, bent toward the ground, then whipped upward, catapulting the squirrel into a neighboring tree. Byte wanted to show her friends how clever the squirrel had been, but the moment was gone. "Byte?" called a voice.

Lost in her thoughts, Byte was barely conscious of the sound. The faint echo seemed miles away.

"Byte!" The voice broke through. It was Mattie.

Byte stopped and turned, surprised to see that she was ten yards ahead of the others. Mattie was bent on one knee, his hand pressed against a tree trunk for balance. He reached down with his other hand and scooped up something from the grass.

"Look," he said. One of the birds, a belted kingfisher, rested limply in his open palm. "It's dead."

Byte ran over to him. She, Jake, and Peter gathered around Mattie to peer at the dead bird.

"It hasn't been dead very long," said Peter. "Bugs haven't gotten to it yet." He prodded it with his finger, turning it over for further inspection. "There's no obvious sign of injury. It must have been sick, or maybe it was just old."

"That's sad," said Byte. She lifted up the bird's limp wing, examined it, then sighed as she smoothed it back into place.

14 "Come over here," Peter called. He had wandered a few yards into the woods. Just as Mattie had, he was kneeling on one knee and staring at the ground.

"What is it?" asked Jake.

Peter looked up, and Byte felt an odd chill when his gaze turned in her direction.

"This is weird," he said. "Here's two more of them. Both dead."

"This doesn't make sense," said Byte, standing next to Peter and staring at the feathered corpses lying in the dirt. "What could be killing them?"

"Maybe it's just a coincidence," said Mattie. "I mean, everything dies."

Peter shook his head. "That's true, but these birds all died recently, and none of them appears to have been injured by predators. That doesn't seem like much of a coincidence."

He slipped his backpack off his shoulders and unzipped it. Byte stared as he pulled out his lunch, slipped a sandwich from its plastic bag, and wrapped it in a paper towel. Using another paper towel he picked up one of the dead birds, placed it in the bag, and squeezed the zipper closed. Watching him, Byte thought of old Frankenstein movies: Peter as the hunchback Igor digging for dead body parts.

Peter paused in his work and looked up at Byte and the others. His hand froze just as he was slipping the wrapped bird corpse into his backpack. Mattie, Byte noticed, had a pinched expression on his face as he eyed Peter's sandwich, the dead bird, the sandwich, the dead bird.

Peter hesitated, catching Mattie's look. "I just want to find out what's killing them," Peter said, as though gathering up dead birds were a common hobby. "Don't you?"

"You know, Peter," said Jake, "you're right. In fact, I was just thinking about that dead raccoon we saw on the side of the road on the way up here. The one with the tire track on it? I think we should call the county coroner's office and—"

Byte swatted Jake's shoulder. "*Jake,*" she said, laughing. "Enough."

Mattie folded his arms accusingly and glared at Peter. "You did that so I wouldn't scrounge off your lunch, didn't you?"

For several moments everyone remained silent, waiting for Peter to complete his task. Then—maybe it was the way the shadows shifted, or the way the breeze swept across her—Byte realized suddenly that Jake was moving away from them, canting his head at an odd angle as though trying to hear something. Byte watched, but soon she could barely see him through the foliage. His figure became a shadow, dappled by the sunlight that streamed through the trees. Curious, she went after him. Peter and Mattie followed, tree branches and dead leaves crackling under their feet. As they approached Jake, he put his finger to his lips. "Listen," he said. "Do you hear that?"

16   Byte held her breath. She heard birdcalls, the trickle of the stream, the rustle of wind in the trees, even the distant wail of a coyote. Then she heard what Jake had heard—a crackling sound from her left, the brush of something against low foliage behind her, and, from the thick grouping of trees just ahead, the crunch of dirt under foot.

"Mule deer?" she whispered. The species was common in these woods.

"That close?" asked Jake. "I don't think so. They'd know we were here by now, and they would have taken off."

Byte caught a flash of color just ahead. A man stepped out from between two trees. He had deep-set eyes and a wispy white beard that trailed along a narrow chin. His skinny legs looked strangely out of place below his thick, muscled chest and shoulders. Another man—perhaps fifty, tall, with hard features and a thin, muscular frame—also stepped into view. He was wearing a red flannel shirt, dirty blue jeans, and grimy leather work gloves.

"What are you kids doing here?" the tall man thundered.

Before anyone could answer, more men crunched through the brush and into view. They seemed to come from everywhere—from ahead of the Misfits, from behind, from either side—perhaps a dozen in all. Each was tall and burly, heavily muscled in the arms and shoulders. The men glared at the four teenagers. One of them carried an ax. Carelessly, as though he were kicking a bit of mud off his shoe, he set the bladed head of the ax against the ground and braced his boot heel against it. Then he yanked upward on the handle so that the head popped off and fell in the dirt.

The forest went silent. Byte no longer heard the bird-calls or the trickle of the stream behind her. All she heard was a rhythmic slapping sound as the man raised up that ax handle and brought it down against his palm, again and again and again.

"I asked you kids a question," said the tall man. "What do you think you're doing here?"

"We—we were just hiking," stammered Peter. "Is there a problem?"

"You're not allowed off the trail," said the man. "You know that. There are signs all over the campground."

You're off the trail too, thought Byte, but she kept silent. The wall of men was suffocating.

"You kids stay on the trail and away from the woods," said the man with the beard. "You hear me? Now get out of here, or there'll be real trouble."

Some of the men looked at one another as though uncertain what to do next. A few stepped aside, leaving an opening in the circle through which the Misfits could leave. The four teens moved slowly toward that opening, glancing at one another, searching for any sign of under-standing in the others' faces.

"Wait a minute!" roared the tall man. "Hold on!" The circle closed again like a cage door. "Before we let them

18 go, I want to know who these kids are and what they're doing here."

The bearded man hesitated. "Zach, don't you think—"

"Shut up!"

Since Peter had been the one to speak before, the man called Zach turned to him now. "I want to see your IDs," he said. He then glared at Byte, Jake, and Mattie. "All of you. Now. Get 'em out."

The three glanced toward Peter, waiting to see what he would do. He was little help. He stood frozen, silent. But Byte could see in his eyes that his mind was working feverishly.

Zach gestured to a man standing behind Peter, who reached for Peter's backpack. He stripped it from Peter's shoulders and tugged at the zipper. When it was open, he peered inside and shook his head. "You were right, Zach," he said to the tall man. He reached inside and took out the lunch bag containing the dead bird. "Look." He tossed the bag into the tall man's waiting hands. Byte noticed that Zach narrowed his eyes. Seeing the bird had clearly changed something—or perhaps it only confirmed something he had already believed.

"Well," said Zach, "look at this. Just out for a little hike, eh?" He shook the bag open, and the dead bird fell into his palm. He flung it into the forest with a sidearm motion. At the same time, the empty bag caught the breeze and fluttered from his fingers, taking off like a kite after its string had broken.

Still rummaging through the pack, the man found Peter's wallet and flipped through the photo windows to study Peter's driver's license and student ID card. A moment later Byte gasped as hands tore the fanny pack from around her waist. Another man locked an arm around Mattie to keep him from running and drew the wallet from Mattie's rear pocket. The man with the ax handle approached Jake.

Soon Zach was glancing through four sets of ID. "Peter Braddock, Byte Salzmann, Jake Armstrong, and Mattie Ramiro." He handed the wallets back as he slowly announced each name, his voice pealing like a bell. Zach nodded a command, and the circle of men spread open. "Get out of here," he said gruffly. "You won't like what'll happen if I see you here again."

The Misfits moved slowly back to the trail. Together they walked in silence toward the distant clearing where they had left their bicycles. Byte watched as Peter turned to glance at the men standing behind them. She stared at him questioningly: *Who were those men? What were they doing? Why did they threaten us?*

Peter shook his head and placed a finger to his lips. *Not now. We'll talk soon.*

The bright clarity of his eyes revealed everything. Peter, Byte knew, didn't have the answers yet, but he was working on them.

"So what was that all about?" Jake asked, tugging at the lock on his bicycle. In his anger he tugged a little too hard, and the vinyl-coated chain whipped through the bike spokes, scoring his knuckle. Mattie bent to yank another strand of sourgrass from the dirt, then stuck it in his mouth, twirling it thoughtfully with his tongue. Byte sat against a tree—legs drawn up, head tilted downward, face hidden behind a mass of hair she combed forward with her fingers.

Peter stood away from the group. He leaned his weight against a tree trunk and stared down the trail, toward the place where, moments ago, the men had surrounded them. The forest sounds seemed distant and subdued— the rustle of wind through branches, the whispered ticking of pine needles blowing off and striking the earth, the faraway laughter of another group of hikers.

"Did you notice," Peter said, as much to himself as to the others, "how dirty their clothes were? Their hands?"

Byte looked at him. "Hmm?"

"You don't get your hands all greasy like that just from hiking. Those men must have been working, using some kind of machinery."

Jake sucked on his scraped knuckle, then wiped it across the leg of his blue jeans. "It could have been pine sap. Could have been anything."

"All over them like that?" asked Mattie. "They would have had to have been climbing the trees to get that dirty." He drew the chewed stalk of sourgrass from his mouth and tossed it to the ground. "Look, so we meet some jerks in the woods. And we *were* off the trail. I say we forget about it. Are we going to let those guys ruin the rest of our day?"

Peter spun around and looked at the others. "No," he said, "we're not." He swung his backpack up onto his shoulder. "Mattie's right. Let's enjoy the rest of the day. But there's one thing I want to do before we leave." He started striding the way they had come, away from the group of men and toward the sun that was falling in the west.

Byte, Jake, and Mattie glanced at one another before following Peter. Byte in particular wondered what Peter had in mind, but she had long ago given up trying to second-guess her friend.

"It's the birds," he finally explained, the uphill walk forcing his breath from him in short bursts. "I thought it was strange…how that guy, the one they called Zach…got all bent out of shape…because of the dead bird in my pack. Why get upset about it? Why bother tossing it away?" Peter had walked so far ahead of his friends, Byte wondered if he knew they could barely hear him now. She watched as he slowed and began walking in a narrow circle just off the trail. "They were here, right?" Peter asked. "I mean, this is where we found them, isn't it?"

Mattie ran ahead and joined Peter. A moment later, all four Misfits were pacing slowly around the clearing, heads down, eyes searching for the other dead birds they had found.

"Hey, look," said Mattie. "Here's where I found the first one." He pointed to a spot on the ground. The earlier rain had muddied the soil, and there, like a fossil in ancient rock, was the light tracing of a bird's shape.

Peter pointed toward some ground foliage. "The others were right over there," he said. "I'm sure of it."

Byte stood in the center of the clearing, her head turning first toward the impression in the ground, then in the direction in which Peter was pointing. Peter and Mattie were right, of course; Byte was certain.

The dead birds should have been right at the Misfits' feet, but they had vanished.

Thoughts of the birds stayed with Byte for the rest of the day and long into the evening. As the Misfits rode their bikes out of the woods, she saw transparent ghost-birds along the trail. Later, as she watched a video with her mom, her mind strayed from the images on the television screen. She saw a belted kingfisher splashing in a stream for fish, and another lying dead at the stream's edge.

Now the digital alarm clock on her bed table blinked red numerals at her, the hour approaching midnight. School tomorrow, she thought, lying in bed, blankets yanked to her chin, eyes fixed on the ceiling. In her mind she relived the day's events: a dead kingfisher lying in the mud, men with greasy fingers and dirty work pants, the slap of an ax handle against a man's palm, echoing. Byte shivered at the images and wrapped the blankets around her more snugly.

Something was happening out there in the woods.

chapter two

the long Formica benches in the Bugle Point High School lunchroom were hinged in the middle. When the school custodians wanted to put them away, the benches folded—like old, hideaway beds—into narrow spaces in the wall.

Mattie Ramiro sat lengthwise on one of these benches, his knees drawn up, his shoulders squeezed into the wall niche. He sat this way often, in effect hiding himself in the crowded room. At four feet eleven and barely ninety-seven pounds, he was probably one of the only students who could fit in the tiny space. The bench was his haven, his thinking spot. If not for the steady chatter from the dozens of students waiting in the snack line, Mattie could pretend that he was alone, or at least that no one could see him.

His backpack lay on the table nearby, and he reached into its outer pouch to withdraw a deck of playing cards. He spread them like a fan, then closed the fan with a

24 sudden flick of his wrist. The top card snapped when he turned it over.

Four of clubs.

Mattie held the card in his right hand and passed the left over it. The card vanished. He passed the hand over again, and the card reappeared. Mattie had found this sleight-of-hand trick in a book and practiced it for weeks. He placed the card back into the deck and shuffled, then, after cutting the cards, fanned them again, this time looking at the backs rather than the faces. He took a deep breath and thought a moment. Then he pulled a card from the deck, turned it over, and smiled. Bingo. The four of clubs. He placed the card into the middle of the deck, cut, shuffled, then snapped off the card from the top. Again, the four of clubs.

Mattie, sighing, stuffed the cards back into their box and slipped them into his pocket. He wasn't in the mood.

The mouth of his backpack lay open, and Mattie spied the corner of his French book, its accompanying workbook, and the spiral notebook that served as his French journal. Seeing these items reminded him of Caitlyn Shaughnessy, who sat next to him in French class. Last week she had been in a rush to leave the lunchroom, so instead of walking over to the trash bin and spitting out her gum, she had tossed it from ten feet away. The trash bin was large and half-empty. It was an easy shot.

She missed anyway.

The wad of chewing gum bounced off the edge of the bin, arced upward, and landed on Mattie's head. Mattie, feeling it land but not yet knowing what it was, slapped his hand down on it hard. He found that he'd pressed a sticky pink wad of Double Bubble into his hair. Caitlyn ran over to him. He remained silent as she sat across from him, studying his head and grimacing at what she saw there. In horror, she clamped her hands down over her eyes. "I am *sooo* sorry," she said. Mattie, realizing what had happened, began tugging at his hair, trying to pull the gum out. "No no no," said Caitlyn. "You'll just make it worse." Her eyes scanned the table, finally falling on Mattie's drink. She pulled the top off and stuck her fingers into the watery cola, fishing out a couple of cubes of ice. "Here…" She sat close to Mattie and held the ice against the wad of gum. Mattie felt chilled water running down his neck.

"What are you doing?" he cried.

"Trust me," she said. She held the ice there for thirty seconds, perhaps a minute. Then she pulled it away, dropped the cubes into the trash, and flicked the water from her fingers. Nodding to herself, she reached for the gum—which was now ice-cold and rocklike—and peeled it easily off Mattie's hair.

As she worked, her face had filled nearly his entire field of vision—like he was sitting in the front row of a movie theater, watching a close-up of Caitlyn as the film's star. Mattie saw pale skin, a small round nose, and a tumble of strawberry blond curls. Mostly he saw her incredible green eyes. Being this close to Caitlyn made him feel as though his feet were slipping out from under him; he had the brief sense that the ground was suddenly a lot farther away than it ought to be.

26   Now nearly a week had passed, and he often found himself glancing over at her during third period, watching her scribble pages upon pages of notes in a spiral-bound notebook, her handwriting composed of large, loopy swirls.

They spoke once or twice, and Mattie learned some things about her: At morning break, she often sat on one of the stone benches in the quad, her nose between the pages of a V.C. Andrews book. Lunchtime she spent with her friends, Latisha Johnson and Amy Li. She took violin lessons. She was a math whiz, cruising through the school's honor track. She carried a Day Runner. She would die if she didn't get on the journalism staff next year. Caitlyn talked the same way she wrote—in long paragraphs.

And yet, as much as he was learning about her, Mattie had not been able to figure out one increasingly important thing: Did Caitlyn Shaughnessy like him, or did she just like to talk?

He squeezed his shoulders together and settled more firmly in the wall niche. The snack line was growing longer. In a few moments, Caitlyn would walk in to buy a drink before heading outside to read her book. Mattie wanted to talk to her, but what could he say? Did she like him? He had no clue. So for now, until he understood more, a voice inside him gave strict instructions: *Don't be an idiot. Let her buy her drink and leave. Say nothing. And later, if she says anything to you in French class, just smile and nod.*

The voice had a point, Mattie thought. The gum incident last week, as astounding as it seemed to him, might have meant nothing at all to Caitlyn. The opportunities for humiliation here were boundless. Yesterday, with perhaps half a dozen pens sitting in his pack, he had asked Caitlyn if he could borrow one of hers—just as an excuse for conversation. Madame Lonstein, the French teacher, had overheard and given him a three-minute lecture on being prepared for class.

Mattie kept his eye on the rear entrance to the lunchroom. Sure enough, Caitlyn Shaughnessy wandered in a few moments later. She was wearing jeans and an oversized Bugle Point High School sweatshirt that hung loose around her shoulders and rumpled at her hips. Caitlyn was one of two freshman class representatives in the student body government. Seeing her now reminded Mattie that this was Spirit Week, and he was not wearing their school colors. He hadn't even spoken to her, and already he was in trouble.

He watched Caitlyn scan the lunchroom, her eyes slipping by Mattie as though he weren't even there. On her second pass, she again looked in his general direction, and this time her eyes locked on him. She waved.

Then she started walking right toward him.

Mattie quickly pulled himself from the wall niche and slid out onto the bench. Caitlyn drew closer, a tattered paperback in her hand and a green nylon backpack slung across her right shoulder. When she arrived at the bench, she heaved her backpack around. "*Ooomph*," she said. It *thunk*ed against the tabletop. The paperback landed next to it.

She plopped down across from Mattie. "Hi," she said brightly.

Without waiting for his reply, she pulled something— a thick elastic band of red fabric—from the pack's outside zipper pocket and began gathering her hair into a ponytail. A quick, practiced motion with her hand circled the elastic around the ponytail's base.

"Hi," replied Mattie.

She glanced at his Levis and gray pullover sweater. "You're not wearing your spirit colors," she said, eyeing him coldly for his offense.

"I know," said Mattie. "I forgot."

Caitlyn planted her elbows on the tabletop and rested her chin in her palms. "I'm bummed."

Mattie sat straighter, painfully aware of how he might appear to her. Did he look interested? Bored? Would a frown right now suggest sympathy—or impatience? He settled on the simplest response: "Why?"

She pulled a folded sheet of paper from her pocket and spread it out on the table. It was last Friday's school bulletin. "Look. We had a Math Club meeting at lunch time last Friday, and I missed it." She shook her head. "It wasn't all that important a meeting. It's the fact that I forgot, you know? It was in the bulletin every day last week. I even wrote it down in my Day Runner." She unzipped her backpack and pulled out her daily planning book. "See? It's right here. 'Friday, 12:30 P.M. Math Club meeting. Room

D-7.'" She slammed the book closed and tossed it onto the table. "I have got to be better organized than this. I've known since I was in the seventh grade that I wanted to get into MIT, right? That's the big math and engineering university in Massachusetts, okay? And to do that, I not only have to be perfect musically, I also have to have all As. I have to. And to get all As, I *have* to be organized. Success is in the details. My dad always says that." She sighed and rested her chin on her hands again. "And to top it off," she added, "they raised the price of drinks from a dollar to a dollar twenty-five, so I don't have enough for my soda."

"I knew about that," said Mattie. "They announced it in the bulletin last week."

Caitlyn's eyes narrowed; she picked up her daily planner and whacked him lightly over the head. "For that," she said, "you now have to say something to make me feel better."

This comment brought a flash of panic to Mattie. He not only had to think of something to say, it had to be the right something. He thought a moment, and a smile slowly spread across his face. He reached into his pocket and pulled out a shiny new quarter. He held it up between thumb and forefinger so Caitlyn could see it.

"Is that for me?" Caitlyn asked, smiling. "That's sweet."

Mattie held the quarter in his right hand and swept his left in a broad, showy arc so that, for a second, the coin was hidden from view. Then he tightened his hands into fists and extended them to her. "It is," he said, "if you can guess which hand it's in."

30   Caitlyn's eyebrows furrowed, then she tapped Mattie's left hand. He opened it, but the hand was empty. She shook her head and tapped the right, and he opened it as well. Nothing. The coin had vanished.

Caitlyn folded her arms and leveled her gaze at him. "All right, so where is it?"

Mattie reached up past her neck and plucked the quarter from her left ear. He held it out to her.

"Oh, that's terrific" Caitlyn said, lightly applauding. "My grandfather used to do that trick with Necco Wafers. Really amazed me when I was five."

Mattie shrugged and held the quarter right in front of her eyes. Then he clapped his hands together, and the quarter vanished again.

This time, Caitlyn threw up her hands. "Okay," she said, "I can see where this is going. I've got two older brothers. They like to grab my purse—you know, toss it back and forth, watch me run around like a little monkey trying to get it." She loaded her belongings into the backpack, smiling, then slung the heavy pack over her shoulder. "Bell's about to ring anyway," she said.

She started to walk away, but before she got very far Mattie called out to her. She turned and gave him a phony glare. "Yes, Mr. Ramiro?" she asked.

"I just thought you might like to know," said Mattie, "that the quarter's in your back pocket."

She stood silent for a moment. Then her hand slapped down on her rear end. When she felt the hard, circular object lodged in the back pocket of her jeans, her mouth flew open, and her face turned a shade of red that was worth far more than twenty-five cents.

Mattie gathered up his own backpack and slipped one arm through the shoulder strap. He glanced to his left, and no more than fifteen feet away stood Byte.

It was clear that she had been watching for several moments. She was leaning against the lunchroom wall, arms folded, computer bag dangling from her shoulder, her smile feigning innocence. Her right foot curled lazily behind the left, and she tapped her toe against the linoleum floor.

Mattie waved a hello to her and trudged over. He caught her throwing a glance at the retreating Caitlyn. She said nothing, but when she looked back at him her eyes were asking all kinds of nosy questions.

"Don't ask," said Mattie.

She shrugged. "I wasn't going to say a thing."

"Because I really don't want to talk about it."

"I understand."

The bell rang ending the morning break, and the two headed off together to third period. Both had math now, and their classes were in the same building. Neither spoke as they left the lunchroom and walked across the quad. Mattie kept his eyes down, hoping Byte couldn't see how red his face was. Finally, after a moment or two of silence, Byte nudged him with her shoulder.

"So," she said, "what's her name?"

"*Byte!*"

She laughed. "Well, I'm sorry. She's cute. I'm just root-ing for you, that's all."

Mattie remained silent and kept his head down as they walked. A large pebble lay on the concrete, and his toe found it. He kicked it so that it skittered ahead of him.

"Okay," he finally said, "her name is Caitlyn."

He knew right away that Byte was waiting for him to say more. When he didn't, she nudged him again. "So, do you like her?"

Mattie shrugged. The answer was yes, but the word that came out was "Maybe." His eyes scanned the other side of the quad, looking for Caitlyn amid the crowd of students. He finally made her out. She strode quickly. *To get away from me?* Mattie wondered. She even stopped for an instant and threw a glance over her shoulder, but she didn't smile at him and she didn't wave. Now she was chatting with some other guy—some really *tall* guy who played on the basketball team. Mattie hadn't a clue what it all meant.

"Hey, Byte?"

"Yeah?"

"Um—is being short like being bald or something?" he asked. "I mean, do girls not like short guys?"

Byte hesitated a moment, then linked her arm through his. They strolled along like an old married couple. "Is Caitlyn smart?" she asked.

"Smart?" asked Mattie. "Yeah, she's really smart."

Byte patted his hand. "Then you've got nothing to worry about."

The E building lay just ahead. Byte unzipped the outer pocket of her computer bag and fished out three folded sheets of paper. Each sheet bore the circle/square emblem of the Misfits, an abstract geometric shape suggesting a square peg and a round hole. Byte gave the sheets to Mattie, and he slipped them into his pocket.

"Peter and Jake need to get these before lunch period," she said. "Can you do it?"

Mattie came to a halt and glared at her.

"Sorry," said Byte. "I wasn't thinking."

Third period. 11:10 A.M.

"Make sure he can't see through that."

"I *am*."

Peter Braddock ignored the voices of his classmates, settling instead into the calm darkness behind the blindfold. He imagined the room in front of him: Michael Takagi, tall and greyhound thin, leaning in the doorway; pale-skinned Aimee Louvier in her black lipstick and black fingernail polish, with black eyeliner accenting her witchlike eyes and long, dark hair cascading past her waist; Marcy Donatello sitting at the desk in front of him, twisting around to watch him, arms crossed on his desktop, eyes peering at him, waiting to uncover the trick.

It was all about the trick.

Peter's father, who was a special agent for the FBI, often played a game with Peter. Observe and deduce.

34 What can you tell about me just by looking at me? Peter had become a master at this game. His father could come home from a day's work, raise his arms in invitation, and Peter would soon know what Nick Braddock had done at work that day, what he had eaten for lunch, what had caused the scratch on his left shoe, or whether or not he had filled his commuter mug at the Shell station on the way home.

Peter's third-period class had finished its work five minutes early today. Their teacher was grading essays, and the students were quietly chatting, waiting for the bell to ring. This moment was a singular opportunity for Peter. Usually he was quiet, removed, relentless in his pursuit of academic success. However, he had come to realize that, to many of the other students, he was little more than a blur passing them on the fast track out of high school and into college. These five minutes, Peter decided, were an opportunity to slow that blur down, to give it—him—clarity and form in the eyes of classmates who did not know him.

So, to reach out, he told them of the Game, and the inevitable challenges had followed.

Michael Takagi had folded his long, winglike arms and said, "Okay, Braddock, prove it." Aimee Louvier had lowered her witch-gaze at him and in a husky voice, said, "This should be interesting." She wore a filmy black shawl over her shoulders, and she whisked it off the way a magician might yank away a silk scarf to reveal the next trick. She folded it to form the blindfold and tied it around Peter's head.

Now the scarf circled Peter's head, its thick knot digging into the back of his neck. "This," said Aimee, "is so you don't cheat."

The rules of the test were simple. Peter would suffer the blindfold for exactly sixty seconds. During that minute, his three classmates would decide which of them would be the subject of Peter's demonstration. They could also use that time to cover up anything they thought might help Peter figure out facts about that person. Peter heard whispering, some shuffling around, then the voice of Michael Takagi.

"Okay, we're ready."

Fingers gripped the knot of the blindfold, tugging the scarf away. Peter blinked in the sudden light, and the first thing he saw was Aimee Louvier leaning toward him, grinning at him almost evilly. "Since you have this magic power—" she said.

"It's not magic," insisted Peter.

She waved his comment away. "Whatever. Since you say you can do this, we're going to start by having you tell us who we picked to be your victim." She leaned back into her desk chair triumphantly.

Peter, unbowed, nodded at the challenge. The question was not all that difficult. Aimee herself was too flamboyant, too obvious and easy a selection. Michael, on the other hand, was too shy. If he had been the one chosen, he'd be doing that nervous habit he had, tugging on his long fingers one by one, cracking the knuckles in each again and again. That left only one choice.

"You picked Marcy," he said.

36 His three classmates looked at one another. Aimee shrugged. "Okay," she said. "You got lucky."

Peter then turned his attention to his subject. He studied Marcy Donatello the way an art student might study a sculpture, gathering detail about her clothing, her jewelry, her school materials, even recalling her earlier behavior during class. "Your mother stayed home from work today," he began. "You're planning on having a burger, chips, and a large drink for lunch. You're worried about a geometry test you're having next period. And, as best as I can tell, last night you got some help in math from Renee Epperstein."

At the first of Peter's observations, Marcy Donatello shrank into her seat. Her fingers clutched her sweater and tightened it around her. When he mentioned Renee, she smacked her palm down against his desktop. "How do you know these things?" she demanded. "Are you following me?"

"Wait a minute," said Michael. "Are you saying Braddock's right?"

"Yes!" said Marcy.

"About everything?" Aimee prodded.

"Yes!"

Aimee tapped a long black fingernail against her cheek. "Okay," she finally said, "did Marcy go to Renee's house, or did Renee go to Marcy's?"

"Renee went to Marcy's," said Peter.

Aimee threw a glance at Marcy, and Marcy nodded.

"And how do you know Renee was helping her?" asked Aimee. "Maybe *she* was helping *Renee*."

"Oh, please," said Peter. "Renee's president of the Math Club."

At that moment the bell rang ending the period, and Marcy Donatello snatched up her belongings. "You're a freak, Braddock," she muttered. She was out of the classroom and down the hallway before Peter could respond. Michael Takagi escaped behind her.

Only Aimee remained. She sat at her desk, eyeing Peter. "You realize, of course," she said, "that you're not leaving here alive until you tell me how you pulled off that little trick."

Peter shrugged and reached for his stack of schoolbooks. "It's not a trick," he said. "I observe and deduce. I happened to notice that Marcy's dad dropped her off at school this morning. Usually her mom drops her off on the way to work, so I figured her mom must be staying home today. As for the lunch, I saw her counting out change on her desktop. She counted out two dollars and eighty-seven cents, then stopped. That's the exact amount the cafeteria charges for a burger, chips, and a large drink. She was checking to make sure she had enough money."

"Okay, I buy all that," said Aimee, "but what about the math stuff? How did you figure that?"

Peter smiled. "Marcy was carrying two geometry books. One of them had Renee's name written along the edge. I figure Renee went over to Marcy's to help her study, and she accidentally forgot to take her geometry book home with her."

"And you knew Renee went to Marcy's, because if Marcy had gone to Renee's—"

38 Peter finished the thought. "Then Renee would be the one carrying two math books today."

Aimee shook her head and laughed. "You just made lucky guesses," she said. "There could have been lots of reasons for Marcy's dad bringing her to school, for her counting the money—for all of it."

Peter frowned. He refrained from saying, *Not really.*

Aimee picked up her book bag and slung it over her shoulder. "You *are* a freak," she said, but she was still smiling as she said it. She turned to leave, but just as she reached the door, she glanced back at Peter with a smile that was both mysterious and teasing. "Oh, and by the way, you're not the only one who knows a few tricks." And with that, she slipped into the corridor.

Peter wondered at the comment until he glanced down and saw the folded paper in his shirt pocket. Scrawled across the paper, in blue ink, was the Misfits' emblem. Mattie must have sneaked it in while Peter was blindfolded. *Byte's handwriting,* he thought. *It's sure to be about what happened in the woods yesterday.*

He tapped the note against his open palm. He didn't have to read it. After years of playing his deduction games, guessing what Byte wanted was easy.

Jake Armstrong found the message waiting for him in his locker. He thought Mattie was slipping a bit, until he realized that the note was tucked in his locker beneath the cover of the textbook he needed for his next class. He envisioned Mattie shoving the note through the locker's tiny air vents, but the paper was folded only in quar-ters—too big for the narrow, three-inch openings.

Once before when Mattie had pulled this stunt, Jake had figured that the little guy had somehow learned the locker combination. He decided, just for fun, to derail Mattie's efforts by replacing the old combination lock with a heavy-duty Master Lock, one that required a key. The new lock, he figured, would turn his locker into a veritable wall safe. Even now, it hung solidly through the hole in the locker handle. Even now, the key to it dangled securely on his key chain.

And even now, of course, Mattie had managed to get past it.

Jake read Byte's note and nodded to himself. *So, we're meeting at lunch. Byte must want to talk about yesterday.* Gathering his books together, Jake stuffed the note into his pocket and stalked off to his fourth-period class.

A fleeting thought came to him just as the bell rang. He hoped he still had the receipt for that stupid lock. He wanted his money back.

When Jake entered the cafeteria, he found Byte seated at one of the tables. She was staring off through the win-dows, crinkling her nose to keep her wire-framed granny glasses from slipping. A computer bag containing her ever-present laptop rested on the table. Near it was a nylon, zippered lunch bag and an open can of Mello Yello.

As far as Jake could see, Byte did not appear to be looking at anything in particular. Her fingers tore off a

40 bite-sized piece from her burger and pushed it slowly into her mouth.

When Jake drew closer, he noticed that the burger patty was light brown in color and dotted with tiny flecks of red and green. "*What* are you eating?" he asked. His eyes squinted a bit as he looked at her, and his mouth suddenly tasted as though it were filled with paste.

"Oh, hi," she said, scooting over on the bench. "I didn't see you coming." She slid her meal over as well, making room for Jake's overloaded cafeteria tray, and she grinned at the question. "It's called a garden burger. It's soy protein and probably some rice mixed with ground-up peppers and other stuff. It's supposed to taste like a hamburger."

"Does it?"

She shrugged. "Sorta kinda almost. Where are the others?"

Jake pointed toward the lunch line. Peter and Mattie had just reached the front of the line and were paying for their lunches. Peter kept looking over his shoulder at Mattie, shaking his finger to make some point while the lady at the cash register waited for him to count out the correct change. In a moment, the two joined Jake and Byte at the table.

Mattie was fuming. "I still think Captain Kirk could whip Captain Picard's butt in a one-on-one fight," he muttered.

Peter slid onto the bench. "Don't tell me," he said. "Let me guess." Without taking his eyes off Byte, he reached down and slapped Mattie's fingers, which had crept across the table to swipe one of Peter's french fries. "You want to talk about yesterday."

"Well," said Byte, "weren't you a little spooked by what happened?"

"Not really 'spooked,'" said Jake. "I'm a little ticked off, maybe. I don't exactly like being ganged up on."

"That's what I'm saying," Byte said. "Something weird's going on out there. Those men were hiding something."

Peter nodded. "Agreed. Did you notice how they acted when they found the dead bird in my backpack? It was as though I had a videotape of them robbing a bank."

"That *was* weird," said Mattie.

"They're doing something," added Peter, "and the key to figuring out what they're doing is the birds. Whatever they're involved in is connected with those dead kingfishers. I'm sure of it."

"That's what I think," said Byte. She looked at Peter, and her voice was firm. "Peter, that forest is important to me. If those men are doing something that's harming the woods—or killing the birds—I want to stop them."

Peter leaned forward and tapped his chin with his forefinger, thinking. "Hmm," he said, "if we want to do that, we're going to have to go back in there." He looked at the others. "At night."

"What are we going to do?" asked Jake.

"Simple," replied Peter. "We're going to find another dead kingfisher." He tossed a french fry into his mouth, swallowed, and slurped at his soft drink. "And then we're going to find out what killed it."

chapter
three

a re we ready?" whispered Peter. He glanced at his friends—at Jake in his black denim jeans and black turtleneck sweater, at Byte in black leggings and black imitation leather jacket. His eyes hovered longer on Mattie—who wore black jeans, yes, but whose black T-shirt sported a neon green Nike swoosh. Mattie blinked his eyes, unknowing, then gazed down at the emblem. "Oh, right," he said. "Okay, so I'm a spy who likes to make a fashion statement."

Peter frowned. "Better turn it inside out. We don't want to take any chances."

Peter disliked leaving anything to chance. Tonight, for example, the Misfits had ridden to Pine Bluff in Peter's restored Volkswagen convertible. They had parked at a tiny building that served as a visitors' bureau and information center, then hiked up the trail to this point. They would complete their mission on foot. Bicycles would not have been safe in the dark, and any noise—the whirr of chain against sprocket, the crunch of dirt beneath knobby tires—might give them away. Each carried a flashlight, a rubber glove in one pocket, and a heavy resealable freezer bag in the other.

Mattie's head poked through the neck of the now inside-out T-shirt. "Ready," he whispered.

"All right, then," said Peter. "We all know the plan. We head up the trail—quietly—and we stick together at all times. Okay, what's the signal if one of us finds a bird?"

Jake held his hands to his mouth and made a fairly decent impression of a birdcall. Peter did the same, then Byte.

"I can't do that," said Mattie.

The others glared at him.

"I'm *sorry*. I can't do birds." He shrugged. "I can do a basketball buzzer—"

"Never mind," said Byte. "Just wave your flashlight. It's a little over a mile to the clearing where we parked our bikes yesterday. I'll lead us there, then we just look around until we find another dead kingfisher and pack it up." She patted the nylon fanny pack attached at her waist. "Simple."

"Right," said Jake. "And then we get out of here as fast as we can." He looked around at the darkened forest, at the black sky and the even blacker shapes of the trees. "I think I'm going to be able to handle that part really well."

Peter nodded. On Sunday afternoon the pine trees had stood tall and green, glistening with the moisture that clung to their needles. Tonight, though, Peter didn't see the beauty in their peaked tops nor the stars through their branches. He saw only needlelike shadows, some blacker than others. All around them, the night sounds of the forest were deafening—the rumble of bullfrogs, the thrum of a million insects, the occasional flutter of bat wings.

"Okay," he said. A deep breath settled the tension from his muscles and steadied his heartbeat. "I think we're ready."

They cupped their fingers over the lenses of their flashlights, cutting the beams and casting a soft, dull glow on the trail before them. Byte led. In fact, she had strayed quite a ways ahead of them. Peter could just make her out as she crept along with her head tilted down, her feet plodding and crunching twigs in the heavy boots she wore.

"Come on," she hissed. "It's not far."

Nothing felt familiar, but after twenty minutes of hiking Peter began to recognize some landmarks. He saw the pine sapling that had scraped his arm as he had ridden yesterday afternoon, the deep rut that had caught his tire and nearly thrown him. Soon they came to the crest of a small hill. Peter remembered tipping his bike over it and coasting roughly toward the clearing where they had rested. Byte was right. They were close, perhaps only a few hundred yards from their target area. Just ahead was the steady rush of the stream.

Behind him, Mattie was grumbling. Peter turned and put a hand up to stop Jake from walking into him, and then glared at Mattie over Jake's shoulder.

In moments they were in the clearing. Byte led them off the main trail, following the streambed and taking

45

them into a thicker part of the woods. Here, tree branches crisscrossed above them, while lower branches brushed their cheeks and scraped their necks. Byte held her flashlight up, and its pale glow brightened only half her face. "The dead birds were right about here," she whispered. "I guess now we just look around and hope we find something."

"We'll cover more area if we split up," Jake suggested.

"Oooh, great plan," shot Mattie. "Then maybe only one of us will get killed. Remember when we split up while we were tracking down the thief who stole that computer chip? Oh, that was sooo much fun."

A half laugh escaped from Byte. "Um—he's right," she whispered. "I don't mind searching for one of these birds, but I don't exactly want to be out of earshot, okay?"

"Okay," said Peter. "Let's look around, then, but stick close. If you can't see at least one other person's flashlight, you've gone too far. Fair enough?"

The glowing faces nodded.

Jake stepped around a tree and let his flashlight beam sweep across the ground in front of him. The others were close by. He could not hear them, but he saw their beams flickering between the trees and across the low ground cover. Mattie stood perhaps fifteen yards away, his beam so low to the ground Jake figured he must be working on his knees. Byte, who was the most familiar with these woods, was ahead of Jake, searching in a

46 deeper patch of foliage. Peter was off to Jake's left, his light arcing across the ground in clean, mathematical circles.

Jake sensed the others' anxiety about this place, even in the way the flashlights jittered in their fingers, but he no longer shared it. He smiled as he remembered Byte's explanation for his ability to remain calm in the midst of danger. Lately she had started calling him the Big Dog. Little dogs, she explained, yap at the door when someone calls or sprint alongside the backyard fence, snarling like wolf pups as a stranger passes. It's all a show. The toughness is a false front.

The Big Dog, Byte went on, doesn't need the show. When the mailman comes up the driveway on a blistering summer afternoon, the Big Dog stays under the porch in the shade, with one eye open. He might let out a single low *woof,* but it's just a warning. It's *I know you're there, and I'm watching you. With one eye. With the other eye, I'm sleeping, because we both know you're not stupid enough to pull anything when there's a really Big Dog right here under the porch.*

Jake's smile lingered as he made another pass over the ground with his flashlight. He knew none of the Misfits wanted to stay in the woods, in the dark, any longer than necessary. So maybe there was a way to hurry matters, to bump up the odds that they would find something.

Jake thought of the bird splashing in the water, fluttering in the spray it had created and rising up with the tiny fish in its beak. Byte had said that the belted kingfisher nests alongside streambeds, and that the female digs trenches in the moist dirt and lays her eggs there.

Perhaps, then, the edge of the stream was the best place to look.

Jake followed the sound of the rushing water until he felt the earth grow soft and muddy beneath his feet. He caught himself just before stepping off the edge of the bank and into the icy water. But which way should he go from here? Downstream would be an easier walk; it would also take him closer to the main trail and closer to his friends. An upstream hike would take more work, would lead him farther from the comfort of his friends' presence and farther from the trail. Jake pondered. Considering the clusters of loud, weekend hikers on these trails, he figured the wiser birds would nest as far away as possible.

As Jake walked, he glanced behind him. The beams of his friends' flashlights grew smaller and dimmer until they burned like distant matchsticks.

He focused his light on the very edge of the stream. Jake walked only about twenty yards before he found a narrow, foot-long trench in the wet soil. Kneeling down so that his nose was right up to the trench, he shone his light along it. He half expected an angry mother kingfisher to leap out and peck at his face, but nothing happened. Inside the trench he found half a dozen speckled eggs, a little larger than jelly beans. Or rather, he found the remains of eggs. Something had gotten to the nest—a lizard or water moccasin, another bird, or maybe a raccoon or a fox. Each egg

48 was cracked through, the inside slurped out like honey from a jar. The head of a baby kingfisher, its eyes closed, lay next to one of the broken eggs.

The important question, Jake knew, was not what destroyed the nest, but why the nest was abandoned in the first place. The belted kingfisher was not tiny by bird standards. Jake figured even a fox would think twice about going after a nest guarded by a healthy adult. So where was the mother? He shone his light around for a few moments and found his answer. A few steps from the nest lay a dead adult kingfisher, its eyes blank and unseeing. Unlike the nest itself, which had clearly suffered an attack from another animal, the adult bird was clean. It bore no scratches, no torn or ruffled feathers to suggest it had battled a snake or blue jay.

Jake tugged the rubber glove from his pocket and slipped it over his hand. Then he drew the freezer bag from his other pocket and scooped the bird into it.

When he finished, he stood and began waving his flashlight in wide arcs to call the others.

The dead kingfisher, sealed in a freezer bag, lay in Jake's palm. His flashlight cast a glow around it, revealing its blank staring eyes and ruffled tail feathers.

"Mission accomplished," whispered Mattie. "Can we get out of here now?"

Byte grinned at Jake. "I second the motion."

Jake handed her the sealed freezer bag containing the dead bird. Byte weighed it in her hand as though it were a fistful of gold dust. "It doesn't weigh anything at all," she said quietly. "There's nothing to it. Such a helpless little thing." Then she unzipped the fanny pack at her waist and placed the wrapped bird inside.

All around them, the forest sounds had grown quieter. Before, Jake had been so focused on his search that he had tuned out the noise. Now his musician's ear caught the difference. The thrum of the crickets, which had been everywhere a few moments ago, seemed far away now, as though the nearby crickets had gone silent. Jake also recalled hearing the ratcheting clicks of raccoons before, but those, too, were gone. He listened closely now, and he heard something crashing through the brush.

"That's a couple of deer running off," Byte whispered.

"Yeah," said Jake, "but running from *what?*"

Twigs crackled. Jake turned in the direction of the sound and caught the glow of a flashlight. A quick scan of the woods revealed three more about fifty sixty yards away.

"We need to get out of here now," he said.

He pushed Mattie so he'd run, but another flashlight—a large one with a six-inch-diameter lens and a heavy battery pack—illuminated the trail as though a car had turned in the direction of the Misfits and clicked on its high beams.

A voice shouted, "There they are!"

"Run!" hissed Jake, but Mattie stood immobile, terrified. A second push from Jake nearly sent him sprawling. "Go!"

The Misfits sprinted down the trail, their flashlight beams ricocheting in a helter-skelter spray of light as they stepped in ruts or leaped over snaking tree roots. The trail was far too treacherous for them to leave the lights off to better hide themselves. Dashing through the woods in the dark was a good idea only to a person who was hoping to break a leg.

Jake, easily the tallest and fastest of the group, raced along in front. He heard Peter following close behind, and knew that Byte, then Mattie, were bringing up the rear. The crackling of twigs became a roar behind them. Jake heard voices calling—deep, men's voices, perhaps more than a dozen of them—yelling again and again: *There they are! Get them!* He ran faster, his ankles twisting slightly each time he planted his foot against a rock or tree root. Pine needles brushed the top of his head and scraped his cheek. Pine sap, sticky and sweet smelling, smeared across his forehead.

A few moments later, he heard a loud, echoing boom, followed by a whistling sound. Someone was firing a rifle at them!

"Go to hell, monkey-wrenchers!" called a voice, and the rifle boomed again. "Go to hell!"

From behind him, Jake heard Mattie's voice cry out, then a branch snapped and something heavy struck the ground.

Mattie...

Jake's tennis shoes scuffled in the dirt as he tried to slow himself. When he stopped, he cupped his fingers loosely over the lens of his flashlight, then sprinted back up the trail, toward the crowd of pursuers. He found Mattie sitting in the dirt, with Peter and Byte already kneeling over him. Mattie's eyes squeezed shut, and he grimaced in pain.

"Oh, my God," whispered Jake, "are you shot?"

Mattie shook his head and almost laughed through his tears. "No," he said. "If I were shot, I'd be dead, *and this wouldn't hurt so much!*"

Jake looked down and saw the problem. Mattie's sneaker was caught in a snarl of tree roots, his ankle twisted strangely.

"I'm stuck," he said.

Peter tugged at Mattie's leg, and the younger boy howled in pain.

"We've got to get him out of here," Peter said, his words punctuated by the shouts of the pursuing men and the glaring flashlight beams that floated against the nearby trees. The thick woods and darkness slowed the men's progress, but they were now only about twenty yards away.

"What do we do?" asked Byte.

Peter looked around—at the trees, at their pursuers, at Mattie's twisted foot. Jake could see him running ideas through his mind, shaking his head slightly as he discarded each one.

Jake looked at Byte and Peter. "Go," he said. "Get out of here. Get the car started, then wait for Mattie and me. We'll be right behind you."

Byte's eyes sparked. "Forget it! We're not leaving you!"

"You won't be," said Jake. "This is the only plan that makes sense, and there's no time to argue. Go!"

Peter and Byte glanced at each other and hauled themselves to their feet. A moment later they were sprinting down the trail.

Jake then turned to Mattie. "Leave it to you," he said, tugging at Mattie's shoelace. In seconds the shoe opened, and Mattie drew his foot out, sucking in a little breath as he did so. Jake hauled him onto his shoulders in a fireman's carry.

"*Oof.* Thanks, big guy," said Mattie.

Jake began a slow jog down the trail, with Mattie holding the flashlight. "Don't thank me," Jake muttered. "You're the one who's going to be helping me with my English homework for the next month."

Monkey-wrenchers.

Jerry Vitale did not like to use those words, or even think them. When Zach had screamed them, blasting out his anger with rifle shots, Jerry had seen the gunfire coming and had dreaded it.

Monkey-wrenchers.

But the explanation seemed possible. When Jerry had shone his light at the intruders, catching them frozen for an instant, he had recognized the faces. Those kids. The same ones from yesterday afternoon. He had yelled at Zach to stop shooting—they were only kids, for crying out loud—but then he had heard those words.

Could they be monkey-wrenchers—and that young? Yesterday he had thought it was odd that they'd stepped off the trail. Most hikers know the rules. Then, when his men discovered the dead bird that the kids had been trying to take out of here…

He shook his head, angry at his own reluctance to see what was right in front of him.

"Okay," he said to his men, "they're gone. Let's head back."

As he turned, his flashlight illuminated something near the edge of the trail just ahead. The object was dark, but bits of it were shiny white, and it glistened in his beam. Curious, he walked over to the object and bent down to examine it more closely.

It was a black tennis shoe, edged with white rubber.

Jerry Vitale reached down with his thick, callused fingers and tugged the shoe from the snarl of roots that held it. He tossed the shoe a couple of feet into the air and caught it as though it were a carnival prize, slipping it under his arm as he walked off with his men.

A single shoe wasn't much, but it was a start. And with it, he might be able to stop those foolish teenagers before somebody got killed.

go, Jake had said. As he ran, Peter remembered Jake's words—and hated himself for obeying them.

He knew that Jake had been right. Sending two people ahead was the most logical course of action. Mattie, injured, could not escape on his own; he needed another person to carry him, and Jake was the largest and fastest member of their group. It also made sense for Peter and Byte to run ahead of their friends, rush to the car, start it, and get it in position at the foot of the trail. Doing so was the best way to ensure that all four Misfits would escape. *Clean, logical, and sensible,* Peter told himself.

But in the back of Peter's mind, in a place very far from Peter's logic and common sense, a voice used the word *coward.*

So Peter ran—and hated himself.

He reached back and locked hands with Byte, dragging her along faster and faster until he could feel her strides getting long and her weight tipping forward. He turned to steady her, to keep her from stumbling, but she had already regained her balance. Instead of falling into his arms as he expected, she plowed into him like a cannon-ball. They fell, a tangled mass of arms and legs, tumbling down the trail. When they rolled to a stop, covered with dirt and pine needles, Peter looked up from the ground to find Byte leaning over him. Her hair hung over her face, and a thin trail of blood ran down her chin from a split lip.

"Are you all right?" Peter asked.

"Come *on!*" Byte shouted. She hauled him to his feet and gave him a shove from behind. The two of them tore down the trail.

Their path ended at the cabinlike visitors' building, where the trail ran down to a narrow wooden staircase. The staircase was four steps high and had a sturdy if weather-beaten handrail. At the base of the staircase was the small asphalt parking lot where Peter had left his Volkswagen.

Peter and Byte clambered down this staircase and shot over to the car. In an instant Peter had opened the driver's side door and popped the seat forward. "You'd better get in back," he said to Byte. His chest heaved from running, and his words were almost lost as he struggled to breathe.

Byte climbed inside, and Peter threw the seat back. Then he slid into the car, started the engine, and mus-cled the stick shift into gear. One quick motion flicked on the headlights, and in another moment Peter yanked the wheel around and stomped on the accelerator. The car's tires spun against the blacktop as it shot out of its parking space.

At the base of the wooden steps, Peter turned off the lights and reached over to open the passenger side door. *There's nothing we can do,* he told himself, *but wait.* Once settled, Peter called an image to mind, willing Jake to run down the steps with Mattie, dump him in the back seat next to Byte, and climb in the front. From his seat, he heard the huffing of Byte's lungs and saw the bursts of fog that blossomed across the rear window as she stared out.

"How long do you figure they'll be?" she asked.

Shortly after he and Byte had started running, Peter had noted that no one seemed to be chasing them any longer. The gunshots had stopped, as had the cries of their pursuers. He saw two possibilities, then: *Those men only wanted to scare us off, in which case Jake and Mattie will arrive in moments. Or the men stopped chasing them because Jake and Mattie were caught, and they're now prisoners of a large group of armed men.*

His only answer to Byte was a quiet "I don't know."

"Maybe one of us should try to find a forest ranger," she suggested.

Peter shook his head. "I don't think we should split up. And what if the others come while one of us is gone?"

They sat in silence. Peter focused on the enginelike hum of the crickets in the woods outside. How often that sound had comforted him, and how terrible and full of threat it seemed tonight, linked as it was to the sounds of men shouting and the crack of a rifle shot.

He soon heard Byte scrambling around in the back seat. He turned and saw her nose pressed against the glass of the window, her hands shielding her eyes from the harsh glare of the halogen lamp that illuminated the parking lot.

"Look!" she cried.

Peter gazed into the woods and could just make out a shadowy figure as it trudged out of the darkness and down the last few yards of the trail. It was Jake, with Mattie slung over his shoulders like a bag of cement. He jogged unsteadily, struggling to keep Mattie balanced. When he reached the stairs and was caught in the light from the halogen lamp, Peter could see Jake's fair skin flushed bright red and mottled. He staggered down the steps, slipped Mattie into the back seat of the car, then collapsed in the front next to Peter and slammed the door shut. He raised his arm and pointed vaguely out through the windshield as if to say "Let's go," but he couldn't find the breath to speak, and the arm flopped back down into his lap as though made of rubber.

"Say no more," said Peter. The Volkswagen roared out of the parking lot.

Byte looked at Mattie. "Are you all right?" she asked.

Mattie nodded. "Ankle hurts," he said, "and my foot's cold." He forced a grin. "No other complaints." He turned to Byte, studying her disheveled hair, the split lip, and the trail of dried blood on her chin. "That's a new look for you, isn't it?" he asked, half-smiling. "It's nice."

Peter came to the stop sign at the main road. Instead of turning left, which would have taken the Misfits away from the forest and toward the city, he hesitated a moment then turned to the right. "What's the plan?" gasped Jake.

Peter tilted his head until he could see Byte's face reflected in his rearview mirror. She caught his glance. "The ranger station?" she asked.

Peter nodded. "I'm pretty sure it's a crime to shoot at people in a national forest," he said dryly.

The narrow, two-lane road brought them to a public campground. Here the road split, one branch taking them into the campground itself, the other bending toward a small wooden building framed with raw pine logs, split down the middle. Above the door in large, aluminum letters were the words U.S. Forestry Service, station #37.

"Will they be open?" asked Mattie.

"They have to have someone on duty around a campground," said Byte, "just in case there's a problem—a campfire gets out of control, someone needs medical attention—"

"Someone gets shot at…" added Peter.

Jake nudged him. "You're taking this whole shooting thing kind of personally, don't you think?"

Peter raised an eyebrow.

He pulled the car up to the front of the building. A single light shone from inside. When he opened the car door, he was struck once again by the power and volume of the forest sounds. Here they seemed less dire, softened by the added sounds of a radio playing rock music, the strum of an acoustic guitar, a woman singing a John Denver song, the titter of distant laughter.

"So, what's going to happen now?" asked Mattie.

"We tell the ranger what happened," said Peter, "then we tell him again, because he won't believe it the first time, then we fill out a report."

Byte suggested Mattie should stay in the car—and off his sore ankle—but Mattie insisted on coming with them. The Misfits found the ranger seated at a desk behind a tall counter. He stood to greet them as they entered, smiling warmly at first, then his eyes traveled over the four of them. Peter suddenly became painfully aware of what the man was seeing: four teens in dirty, torn clothing, their faces scratched by branches and smeared with mud and pine sap, Byte's mouth bleeding, Mattie leaning against Jake.

"Can I *help* you?" he asked.

He was not terribly tall, perhaps a bit taller than Peter, and thinner than Mattie in build. He appeared to be quite young, but his dark hair was already receding, brushed straight back and slicked with styling gel into a gleaming widow's peak. Though the sleeves and cuffs of his clothing were the right length, Peter had the vague sense that the man's uniform did not fit him—or better, did not *suit* him. The man gave the impression of being too thin, too weak to be a law enforcement officer.

"Ranger…Tummins," said Peter, glancing at the man's badge, "we need to report an incident."

"We were chased out of the woods," added Jake, "by a group of men. One of them shot at us with a rifle."

The ranger's eyes widened. He quickly grabbed a pad of report forms from beneath the counter and asked each of the Misfits for personal information—names, addresses, phone numbers—then he came to the part of the form where he had to describe the actual event.

"Where did the incident occur?" he asked.

"The east trail," said Byte, "above the stream, just short of Pine Bluff. We were walking along, and they just…"

At the words Pine Bluff, the man froze. The pen in his hand left a dark squiggle across the center of the page. He very slowly set the pen down and placed the pad of forms back beneath the counter. "You kids were out by Pine Bluff?" he asked, his tone suddenly flat and even.

"Sir?" said Peter.

The ranger's tone face grew darker and full of threat. "I asked you a question. Were you or were you not out by Pine Bluff?"

"Yes, we were," said Byte, "and the men—"

The ranger interrupted. "You were off the trail, then. Didn't you see the signs—or are they not teaching you to read in school anymore?"

Looking stunned, Byte paused. "We…we know we're not supposed to be off the main trail," she offered weakly, "but—"

The ranger roared at her. *"Don't ever go off the main trail!"*

Peter's mind swayed. Flabbergasted by the man's reaction, he struggled for a little bearing. "Sir?" he asked. "I don't think you understand. Ranger…uh, Tummins, you see, these men had a rifle, and they—"

The ranger's hand smacked down on the countertop. The sound echoed like gunfire. "If you can't obey the

rules," he shouted, his voice high and wavering, "you
shouldn't be hiking these trails. I ought to cite you kids
right now. Now get out!" He glared at them, his cheeks
huffing in and out like tiny bellows. The Misfits looked
at one another and silently made their way to the door.

Once outside, Peter felt Jake's hand clamp down on his
left shoulder. "Is it me," Jake whispered, "or did we just
meet the Barney Fife from hell?"

Peter shook his head. "Not here. Wait till we're in the
car."

"I figure there are two explanations for what we just
witnessed," said Peter. He steered his VW out of the
campground area, toward the road leading back to the
freeway that would take them back to Bugle Point.
"Either we've walked into something we shouldn't have,
or Ranger Tummins just happens to be a little bent."

"Are you going to tell your dad what happened?" asked
Byte.

"Not likely," Peter answered. "He's in law enforcement,
so he'll automatically side with Tummins. He'll want to
go after the guy with the rifle, of course, but he'll also
jump all over my case." Peter affected a voice that was
more forceful, more commanding than his own. "'You
were where?' he'll say. 'Doing what?' Then he'll do
this…" Peter held up his empty, open hand in a gesture
imitating his father, "and wait for me to hand him my
car keys."

"Ouch," said Mattie. "So what do we do?"

Peter shrugged. "Come back tomorrow, I guess. Show up earlier in the day and hope that a different ranger is on duty, so we can file that report."

"If it will do any good," Mattie added.

As he drove, Peter explored other aspects of the evening's events: What was killing the birds? And what was so important about them that a group of men would potentially kill to hide the answer?

"Oh, shoot," Byte said.

Peter glanced in the rearview mirror and saw her reaching inside her fanny pack, drawing out the plastic freezer bag containing the dead kingfisher. A tiny explosion of loose feathers came with it. "The freezer bag split. Must have happened when we fell, Peter."

The bird, still wrapped in plastic, rested in her palm. She touched a fingertip to the crest of gray feathers sweeping up from the crown of the bird's head. "Poor little thing," she cooed. She stared at it, running her finger along the length of its delicate body. "So, Peter," she finally said, still lost in her examination of the bird, "what's the next step? I mean, what do we do with this little guy now?"

"Well," said Peter, "we'll have to find someone who can tell us what killed it—do an autopsy or something. In the meantime, one of us will just have to keep it frozen at home."

Jake, Byte, and Mattie glanced at one another.

"Hmm," said Jake. "Dead rotting bird next to tomorrow's hamburger. Yum. Who thinks that keeping the bird is a job for our fearless leader?" He raised his hand.

Two other hands went up. Neither belonged to the "fearless leader" himself.

"What?" said Peter. "You've never had a dead animal in the freezer before?"

Once home, Peter found a replacement for the broken freezer bag. He carefully rewrapped the bird and slipped it into the back of the kitchen freezer, right behind the giblets from last Thanksgiving's turkey that his mom had cooked and never gotten around to using. He was careful to position it far from the rainbow sherbet. Every time his dad came home with a video rental, the sherbet was the first thing his parents grabbed.

Later that night, when the clock crawled to the 11:00 P.M. mark, his mother began tossing him her patented don't-you-have-school-tomorrow look, and Peter dragged himself off to bed. He lay awake, watching light from a street lamp slice through a tiny opening in the blinds, and he tried to draw conclusions from the little information the Misfits had gathered. Kingfishers were dying from an unknown cause. The men prowling in the woods were aware of the kingfishers' plight and were concerned that the Misfits knew of it as well. Also, the men were eager to protect themselves from discovery— so eager that they would shoot at the Misfits, and kill them if necessary. Lastly, Ranger Tummins was unwilling to help the Misfits pursue the men who had shot at them.

The men in the woods were consistently ready to pounce on anyone too interested in the dying kingfishers.

64 They might well be responsible for what was happening to the birds. Or not. And Ranger Tummins was extremely upset once the Misfits told him where they'd been when the men shot at them. They had been off the trail, but why would their exact whereabouts be more important than the attempted shooting? Tummins was involved as well. Or not.

That was the trouble with this case so far, Peter decided. Too few facts available, too many conclusions with "or nots" attached.

He stretched out his legs and spread his arms across the width of the bed. Moments later, his eyes closed, and his breathing grew slow and deep. He slept soundly, dreaming that he ran through a tunnel and that shadows stretched out of the dark, reaching for him as he passed.

Peter?

A voice and a dull knocking sounded from someplace very far away. Or maybe it wasn't so far; maybe the sounds were close, but muffled.

"Peter, wake up."

Peter forced his eyes open to see a figure standing in his bedroom doorway—his father, Nick Braddock, in pajamas and bathrobe, hair mussed from sleep, body rigid as a monument. Light spilled in from the hallway, illuminating the thin but muscular man from behind and casting him in silhouette.

"Dad?" mumbled Peter. He reached for his glasses and unfolded them, then glanced at the glowing numerals on his alarm clock. It was 1:15 A.M.

Nick Braddock stepped forward, and half his face caught the glare from the street lamp. Peter saw the tight muscles in his father's jaw.

"Better get up, son," Mr. Braddock said.

Peter followed his father downstairs. Peter's mother stood in the living room—thin, disheveled, her face pale and her arms hugging her body. She remained silent, gazing at Peter.

In a moment, Peter understood why. Three men stood in the room with her.

The first had the build of a professional football player, and he had shaved his hair close to his head in military style. He wore a navy blue suit that, in spite of its cut, could not hide the telltale lump at his armpit: He was wearing a shoulder holster. The size of the lump, Peter decided, indicated that the weapon was even larger than Nick Braddock's 9mm Glock. Peter recognized this man as FBI Special Agent Robert Polaski. Agent Polaski worked in the same office as Peter's father, and the two had often worked cases together. At this moment, Polaski's face was void of the warm smile Peter had seen on so many occasions and held the stern, flat look of a working FBI agent.

The second man stood much taller than Peter, his thin body heavily muscled and his features sharp and angular. Peter gazed at the man's arm, at its coat of curly black

66 hairs, at the way the muscles moved thick and ropelike beneath the skin as the man clenched one hand. A moment later, Peter remembered where he had seen the man's face. This was the leader of the men in the woods, the men who had encircled the Misfits and taken the bird from them.

The last man shuffled his feet nervously. With his slicked-back hair and Forestry Service uniform he was instantly recognizable.

"Hello, Ranger Tummins," said Peter, "and Agent Polaski." He turned his gaze back on the man from the forest, waiting to see what would happen next.

"Nick," said Agent Polaski, "Mrs. Braddock—" Peter noted the deferential tone in the way Agent Polaski greeted his parents. It almost sounded as though he were apologizing for what he was about to do. "We're investigating a complaint that your son, along with three of his friends, entered the national forest earlier tonight and…" Somehow he ran out of breath before reaching the end of his sentence. He paused and took another gulp of air. "…and trespassed off the trail." He turned toward the man with the barrel chest. "Is this who you saw, sir?"

The man nodded. Nick Braddock shot a look at Peter that cemented Peter's growing sense that he was in a good deal of trouble.

"Ranger Tummins, is this the young man who came into your station about four hours ago and identified himself as Peter Braddock?"

Tummins remained silent with his eyes on the floor, but nodded a yes. "Is that was this is about, Bob?" asked

Nick Braddock. "You wake us up at one in the morning because Peter wandered off the trail?"

Polaski shook his head. "No—no, it's a little more than that."

"We have reason to suspect," said Ranger Tummins, "that your son, or one of his companions, may have taken something from the woods when they left."

So that's it, Peter thought. They knew about the bird—or they had guessed. He wanted to tell Agent Polaski and Ranger Tummins about the behavior of the men—the way they had threatened the Misfits Sunday afternoon, the fact they had shot at the Misfits earlier tonight—but he held his tongue. These men had gathered behind them the power and authority of both the U.S. Forestry Service and the Federal Bureau of Investigation. Peter didn't know what the men in the forest were doing, but they had certainly managed to protect themselves.

The thick-chested man tossed an object in Peter's direction. Peter, off guard, threw up his hands to catch it. It was a black tennis shoe with white rubber trim.

"Don't deny it was you, kid," said the man, "or we'll just gather your friends together and play Cinderella with that shoe."

Peter nodded. Setting the sneaker down on an end table, he walked to the kitchen, reached into the freezer, and grabbed the dead bird. He returned with it to the living room and handed it, without a word, to Agent Polaski.

"Trespassing off the marked trail," said Ranger Tummins, his tone, like Polaski's, embarrassed, "is an infraction. Removing fauna, living or dead, is a misdemeanor, um, under federal law. However, since the boy has been so cooperative and returned the bird, the Forestry Service doesn't see any reason to pursue the matter further."

The three men turned and headed toward the door. The tall man went first, followed by Tummins. Agent Polaski went last. As the agent turned to close the door behind him, Nick Braddock's arm flashed out and stopped the door from closing.

"What's going on here, Bob?" he whispered.

Polaski turned and looked at him. His face revealed nothing. "Nick," he said, "it's over. Just leave it alone."

"Leave it—?"

The door shut with a loud click.

Without a word, Peter's father turned to Peter with hand extended, waiting for the car keys to drop.

He returned to bed and lay on his back, his hands folded behind his neck and his legs crossed at the ankles. The only certainty now was that he had to reach at least one of the other Misfits, had to get word out about what had happened tonight and begin making plans for tomorrow.

Who could he call? The logical choice was Jake. Jake often complained about being a light sleeper, and, like Peter, he had a phone extension in his bedroom. Chances were good that Peter could call, even at this hour, and Jake would pick up the phone before either of his parents knew it was ringing.

He picked up the phone and punched in Jake's number. The voice that came back to him was dull with sleep.

"Hullo?"

"Jake? Peter. Listen." Peter cupped his hand around the mouthpiece and spoke quietly, so as not to bother his parents. "We need to meet tomorrow. I don't know what's going on, but this whole deal just turned nasty. We're into something that's way over our heads. We're going to need help."

chapter five

Tuesday afternoon

rebecca Kaidanov tapped out the last few lines of her article. The assignment was a puff piece, half a column related to the upcoming congressional election. The two candidates would arrive in Bugle Point tomorrow, meet with reporters throughout the day, and square off in a televised debate that evening.

Rebecca would cover none of those events. Instead she struggled with feelings of humiliation as she finished her current assignment—a story about a puppy one of the candidates had adopted from a local animal shelter. Rebecca sighed. At least the candidate, Megan Warwick, had allowed a few questions at the end of the photo op. Rebecca had been able to slip in a couple; she had even hurled a curveball or two at one of the campaign staffers as the group hurried off.

She thought about the campaign and how it had become so much tighter than anyone expected. Victor Madison, the elderly incumbent, had served his congressional district for twelve straight terms, becoming, in the process, a tough political veteran and a key leader of several congressional committees. His opponent, Megan Warwick, had appeared from nowhere—unknown, smiling, quick-witted in front of the press, charming voters as she hammered Madison for his poor record on environmental issues. Polls showed the two candidates in a virtual dead heat.

Rebecca typed furiously. Her dog story was slated for page five of tomorrow's paper, just above the chart showing this week's Wingo numbers. She shook her head. Maybe with a little begging she could get Mac, her editor, to run the story on page two.

Well—maybe page three.

She tore the hard copy from the printer and scooted her chair away from her desk. Her "office" was an eight-by-ten modular cubicle marked off by walls of particleboard. Dense fabric covered these walls, making them look like bulletin boards in an elementary schoolroom. Rebecca had stapled all over them notes from different stories she was covering. On her desk sat a framed award for a feature she had written about children in Chechnya. To her right hung a Doonesbury cartoon, yellowed and tattered, clipped years ago from a Sunday comics page.

Centered above the desk was a photograph of a man. He had a thick gray beard and eyes that were tired and red rimmed. Dark pouches lay beneath those eyes, telling of the man's weariness, but tiny wrinkles edged his mouth—a smile so faint only Rebecca would recognize it. The man was Anatoly Kaidanov, her father, who had been a reporter in the old Soviet Union.

With the completed article in her hand, Rebecca rushed to her editor's office. Ron McLaren—Mac—would be leaving soon, and Rebecca wanted him to see the story before he left and perhaps nudge him into placing it nearer to page one. She found him in his office, his tall frame lolling in his chair, his stocking feet resting on the desktop. He spoke into a phone propped between his shoulder and ear and waved Rebecca in.

"We're not responsible for what comes out of the mayor's mouth," he was saying. "He knew he was on the record." He glanced at Rebecca and made a twisting motion with his hands, as though wringing water from an old rag. It was his way of telling Rebecca that the caller was squirming. Rebecca understood why. Sometimes the mayor, when caught off guard, made statements to a reporter that he later regretted. "Our reporter has it on tape.... How could it be taken out of context? It was the only comment the mayor made." He waved at Rebecca, signaling her to show him the pages she had brought. He looked over them while the person on the other end of the line continued to speak. "Uh huh.... Uh huh. Well," he said, "maybe the mayor should have second thoughts *before* he says something foolish in front of a reporter."

A loud buzz sounded from the receiver as the person on the other end of the line shouted a final threat. Then silence. Mac hung up the phone and continued to study Rebecca's pages.

"There's nothing more pitiful," he grumbled, "than a politician who gets caught saying what he really thinks."

Mac's face revealed nothing as he read Rebecca's article. His eyes ran along the lines of text like a daisy wheel from an old printer—cool, mechanical, emotionless. Rebecca had once watched him read a colleague's Pulitzer prize–winning story on the vanishing rain forest, only to toss the pages aside and remark "nice piece." These were the highest words of praise Rebecca had ever heard the man utter.

"This little tag line at the end, the one about Warwick's debate strategy. Did her aide confirm it?" he asked.

Rebecca shrank a bit under the question. "Well—yes. In a way."

"In a way?"

"Well," said Rebecca, "when I asked, she nodded. And when I said, 'Is that a yes?' she nodded again and walked away."

Rebecca winced as Mac drew a red pencil from his shirt pocket and lined out two sentences.

"Mac, the story is good—" Rebecca stopped in mid-sentence, although the editor said nothing, just gazed at her steadily.

His expression said it all. "Look at this face I'm getting," she said. "There's no point in talking to this face, is there?"

"None at all."

Rebecca grabbed an office chair and swung it around to face her boss. She sat, her elbows jammed onto his desktop, her chin resting in her hands. "Mac," she said, "when are you going to give me some real news to report?"

His eyes never rose from her manuscript pages.

"Anyone who wants to be a reporter is either an idiot or a masochist," he said.

"Or an idealist. And don't patronize me. I'm a good writer."

He looked at her. His eyes stayed on her a long time, long enough that she could almost read the man's thoughts: *How badly does she want this? Where can she do the best job?* And, most importantly, *Is she ready?*

"You're a good feature writer," he told her. "One of my best. Why do you want to switch to hard news?"

She opened her arms wide in an expansive gesture that seemed to reach through the office window and draw in everything—Bugle Point, the Pacific Ocean, the world. "Because things are happening out there!" she cried. She wanted to say more but couldn't. Even after all these years, her second language failed her when the feelings were complex. At stressful moments, her native Russian seized her tongue and kept her from phrasing her thoughts in English.

Mac leaned forward and steepled his fingers. He said nothing for a few moments, just tapped his fingertips together, punctuating his thoughts. "You know," he finally said, "I met your father in 1972. It was my first year as a reporter. He was giving a speech at the UN."

Rebecca remembered the speech. Her father had been a newsman in the old Soviet Union, working for Pravda, the country's largest newspaper. In Russia at that time, the government controlled the newspapers. The government decided which stories were "news," which headlines would see print, and which events "never happened." Her father was loyal for many years, writing what the government told him to write. But each time he wrote a lie, Anatoly Kaidanov would literally be sick to his stomach. When Rebecca was a teenager he was arrested, condemned to Lubyanka prison, then finally released. In 1991 he fled with Rebecca to the United States.

Rebecca crossed her arms along the back of the chair and rested her chin on them. "You know," she said quietly, "I don't believe I ever told you the whole story—I mean, what my father did that got him in so much trouble."

"No," said Mac. "You never did."

Rebecca smiled at the memory. "The Soviet President, Yuri Andropov, was very ill. He was close to death, but the government would not allow the newspapers to say so. They printed stories saying 'Andropov Recovering,' or 'Andropov Returning After Minor Illness.'"

As she spoke, Rebecca picked up a pencil from Mac's desk and began turning it over in her hand, studying it.

"Well, my father's integrity as a journalist would not allow him to live any more lies. I remember him stalking through the house, muttering under his breath through the evening newscast. I did not understand it at the time.

"When Andropov finally died, front-page headlines were everywhere. The whole world knew the leader of the Soviet Union was dead. Two days after the funeral, my father printed a small story, hidden in the back pages of *Pravda*. Its headline was 'Doctors Say Andropov Just Suffering From Head Cold.'"

Mac chuckled and shook his head. "He was quite a

guy—and a great reporter. There's a lot of him in you, Rebecca."

"I know," she said. "He was very obstinate, and so am I. So, do I get to do some hard news?"

Mac laughed. "In time. For now, you get page five."

Peter and Mattie entered the *Courier* office building. Mattie watched the whirlwind of activity and found himself thinking of an ant farm he had once owned as a child. The newsroom was immense, lit by huge banks of fluorescent lights in the ceiling. Phones jangled a dozen at a time. Behind the jangling, the voices of reporters, photographers, and editors overlapped in a wash of background noise.

"Hmm," said Peter, observing the scene. "It's hard to know where to begin."

"Are we looking for someone in particular?" asked Mattie.

"Not necessarily."

Mattie pulled a quarter from his pocket and set it across the back of his hand. With a practiced motion of his fingers, he rolled the coin back and forth, a one-handed dexterity trick that had required weeks of practice. "So," he said, "tell me again why we need to talk to a reporter."

"Freedom of the press," said Peter. "A reporter can get away with asking questions we can't. A reporter has the name of a newspaper or magazine standing behind him. A reporter can go places we can't."

Mattie frowned. "Well—suppose the person doesn't *want* to answer a question. Then the reporter isn't any better off than we are."

Peter raised his index finger. "Aha," he said, "that's the beautiful part of it. A reporter can write up a news story *whether or not* the subject of the story wants to cooperate. Most people will answer a reporter's questions because they want their side told."

Oops—right, thought Mattie. Earlier, when the Misfits had met at school, Peter had said pretty much the same thing—only Mattie, daydreaming about Caitlyn Shaughnessy, had barely heard.

They walked across the newsroom, making their way around the tiny office cubicles like mice in a laboratory maze. Most of the people they saw were speaking into telephones or typing furiously into computers. A few glanced up as the teenagers passed. One young man wearing a sweater vest and a bow tie ran through the office, clutching sheets of paper that crackled in his hand as he sped by.

Peter called to him. "Excuse me? Can you tell us who we see about a news story?"

The man looked at the two teenagers, clearly assessing whether or not the question was a waste of his all-too-valuable time. He paused, threw an impatient gesture toward an office cubicle, and stormed off.

Mattie walked to the cubicle and waved Peter to join him. On the cubicle entrance was a plastic nameplate held in place by tiny brass screws. The nameplate said Rebecca Kaidanov, Features. The cubicle was empty.

"Well," he said, motioning to the workspace, "here's a start. Somebody must work here."

The computer on the desk was running, but a screen-saver had kicked on. Brown liquid—coffee, most likely—formed a thin, almost imperceptible ring next to the mouse pad.

Peter stared intently at the workspace, and Mattie sensed he saw far more in the clippings, the Post-it notes, and the messy desktop than others would. But Peter didn't offer any information; he just yawned, took off his glasses, and wiped the lenses, saying, "She'll be back shortly."

Mattie frowned. "How do you know?"

Moments later a young woman approached the cubi-cle, steam swirling from the white mug in her hand. She wore jeans and a long-sleeved, white blouse. Her coarse black hair hung in a clump at the back of her neck, twirled around a pencil. She strode past Peter and Mattie, nodded a greeting, and plunked the mug down on the desk, splashing a few drops of hot coffee across her hand.

Mattie grinned and threw a look at Peter. *Right again.*

"Ow," said the woman, reaching for a tissue. "Can I help you?"

"Your nameplate here says 'features,'" said Peter. "Do you cover news stories?"

"Depends," she replied. "Do you own a puppy?" Peter and Mattie looked at each other. The reporter made a dismissive wave. "Never mind." She shook Peter's hand, then Mattie's. "Rebecca Kaidanov. What can I do for you?" Mattie noted the odd way the woman pronounced her vowels, the hard way she clicked off the *K* in her last name.

Peter handed her a business card.

misfits **inc.**
investigations

Mysteries are no mystery to us!

Jake Armstrong   Matthew Ramiro
Peter Braddock   Byte Salzmann

"Misfits, Inc., huh?" said Rebecca. Her hair tumbled down as she drew the pencil from it. She then stuck the pencil into an electric sharpener on her desk, and the sharpener made a dull humming sound, not the shrill grinding of motor-driven blades Mattie expected. The reporter tossed the pencil onto her desktop and reached into a drawer for another. "Sorry," she said. "I keep forgetting the sharpener's broken. Okay, let's get started."

She took notes as Peter told her of the events in the forest, beginning with the discovery of the dead kingfishers.

80 As Peter spoke, Mattie found himself transfixed by the reporter herself. Rebecca Kaidanov's dark hair, her pale, almost translucent skin, and her square but delicate jawline were a striking combination. Mostly Mattie noticed the reporter's eyes, which were sea-blue and held a hint of amusement.

Mattie reached into his pocket for the multi-tool he always carried and, while the reporter was focused on Peter, he reached behind her for the wounded pencil sharpener. Mattie popped off the plastic tray that caught the shavings. *Hmm—just as I thought*, he mused. The tray was packed full and the shavings had spilled into the device, hampering the turning of the blades. He emptied the shavings into the wastebasket. Inside the machine, he also found two loose screws, the ones that secured the motor and allowed it to spin properly. Mattie used his multi-tool to tighten the screws, then replaced the plastic tray and returned the sharpener to the reporter's desk. Rebecca was scribbling notes.

As Peter finished the account of the events in the woods, she frowned at her notepad. "The story seems a little thin," she said. "I'm not sure what I can do."

"There's more," said Peter. He told her how the FBI and the Forestry Service had appeared at his door, and how they had confiscated the dead bird. The reporter sat a little more upright and began scribbling a little faster.

"Can you give me names?" she asked.

Mattie smiled as Peter rattled off the names, the correct spelling of the names, the badge numbers of Ranger

Tummins and Agent Polaski, and the make, model, and license number of the car they had arrived in. The reporter wrote down the information, thoughtfully tapping her pencil against the desktop when she finished.

"Why all the fuss over a dead bird?" she asked. "And why involve the FBI?" She opened a desk drawer and withdrew a small stack of business cards. She handed one to Peter. "I will try to look into your story, but I cannot make any promises. If anything else happens that might be connected, make sure you call me."

Peter hesitated a moment, then took the card and slid it into his wallet. He looked at Mattie, clearly struggling to hide his disappointment—and failing. The two of them rose to leave.

"This isn't over yet," he muttered as they headed for the door.

Rebecca watched the two boys leave, then gazed down at the business card Peter had given her. *Misfits, Inc.? Investigations? Great. Teenagers with delusions of grandeur.* Still, she considered, the boy had provided so much detail. If he was making all this up, he'd have to have a pretty remarkable imagination. Perhaps it wouldn't hurt to put him to the test.

She reached to a small shelf unit behind her and grabbed the Bugle Point phone directory, flipping to the blue pages in the center that marked the government listings. *City…state…federal…* Her polished fingernail landed on a listing near the bottom of the page. *Federal Bureau of Investigation, Bugle Point office.* She grabbed the phone and quickly punched in the number.

"FBI," said a voice. "Agent McNab."

"Agent Robert Polaski, please," said Rebecca.

"One moment."

Rebecca heard the click of a hold button. After a few moments of silence, another voice came on the line.

"This is Special Agent Polaski."

Rebecca introduced herself and identified herself as a newspaper reporter. She wanted Polaski to know that he was speaking on the record and that anything he said might appear in print. "Agent Polaski," she began, "we have a report that you made an on-duty call early this morning at the home of Nicholas Braddock, a fellow FBI agent. What was the purpose of that call?"

The lengthy pause that followed her question spoke volumes to Rebecca. She figured Polaski was running the event through his mind, undoubtedly trying to determine what she knew, what he could safely deny, and what information Rebecca could confirm from other sources.

"Special Agent Braddock is not under investigation," he said icily. "Other than that, I have no comment."

"Agent Polaski," said the reporter, "why are the FBI and the U.S. Forestry Service knocking on people's doors in the middle of the night to confiscate the remains of a dead bird? What's this about?"

The agent waited a much longer time now before answering. "Ma'am," he said, his voice flat and threatening, "the FBI neither confirms nor denies your story. I have nothing else to say."

Rebecca heard a click and then a dial tone.

She smiled. She had no clue what was going on, but she darn well knew she had a story. And once she knew more, Mac was darn well going to let her write it.

She tapped her pencil against the desktop again, this time breaking the point. Without thinking, she thrust the pencil into her sharpener and was startled to hear the machine grind like a well-tuned motorcycle. She yanked the pencil out and stared at its new, finely sharpened point.

Now how did that happen? she wondered.

"They call themselves Foxfire," said Byte. "They're some kind of radical environmental group. I discovered them on the Net, e-mailed them, and found out they were local. They said we could stop by."

She and Jake sat in Jake's powder blue Ford Escort. Byte had just shanghaied Jake, locating him in the student parking lot after school and leaping into his car before he'd had a chance to object.

"You're driving," she'd said.

The journey had taken them away from downtown Bugle Point and into an old, dilapidated area of the city. Cracks and potholes marred the road, causing Jake's tires to make rhythmic thumping sounds as they pounded into each one.

84   Foxfire's address had not been displayed on their Web site. And when Byte called them, the group's members, whoever they were, had seemed anxious—if not down-right paranoid—about revealing their location. Byte had spent most of her fifth-period class, where she served as a library aide and Internet tutor, chatting online with a member and trying to win his confidence.

"So these environmentalist guys," said Jake. "How'd you get them to trust you?"

"Oh," said Byte, "they quizzed me. You know—who was the captain of the Exxon *Valdez,* what's the worst contributor to global warming, what was the Kyoto Agreement—simple stuff like that."

"*Simple?*" cried Jake. He shook his head. "If we find them, you're doing the talking."

"I can see it," said Byte. She pointed at an apartment building, its bricks chipped and sun-faded.

Jake pulled over and parallel parked on the street. Inside the complex, a narrow flight of stairs led them into a dark, second-story corridor. Above them a ceiling light flickered, went out, then spat a small fountain of sparks before coming back on. Byte followed the brass numbers marking the apartment doors, stopping only when she looked up and found a tiny, whirring video camera staring at her from above a door frame.

"Must be the place," she said. She rapped twice, loudly.

A male voice, crackling with static, blared from a radio speaker mounted near the doorknob. "Who is it?"

At the gruff sound of the voice, Jake stepped a little

closer and interposed his huge frame between Byte and the door.

"It's Byte. We talked over the Net, remember?"

Byte heard a rattling, the metallic scrape of a security chain drawing back, followed by the click of a lock. The door opened to reveal a young man with a full, curly shock of carrot-colored hair. Byte had to force herself not to stare. A wispy goatee hung limply from his chin, and dark freckles dotted his face and arms. He was tall— several inches taller than Jake, who was six foot two— but he was also unbelievably thin, his waist seemingly no bigger around than Jake's muscular thigh.

"You didn't say the friend you were bringing was a guy," he said, clearly disappointed. "Come on in." He turned around and went back into the apartment. Byte watched the bend of his knees as he walked and thought of circus clowns teetering on stilts.

Inside, a second young man sat at a computer. When Byte and Jake entered, he moved to a corner of the apartment and sat on the floor, his back leaning against the side of a desk. A veil of fine blond hair swept down past the tip of his chin, and he took a lock of hair between his thumb and forefinger and began to chew it.

The last member of Foxfire—or at least the last one in the apartment at the moment—was a young woman. She was thin and sharp featured, her sandy-colored hair pulled into a severe ponytail. She wore camouflage green trousers with a large, pleated, snap-down pocket on the outer thigh, just above the knee: army jungle fatigues purchased from a military surplus store. Her top was a plain khaki T-shirt. She swung around now to stare at Byte and Jake, a brittle and faintly disapproving look on her face. Something about her manner suggested she was the leader of the group, or at least the one who needed impressing, so Byte handed her one of the Misfits' business cards.

"Misfits, Inc.," read the woman. "Well, meet Foxfire." She gestured toward the tall young man. "This is Terry Summers." Then she motioned at the man with hair in his mouth. "Paul McBride. And I'm Carol Jablonsky."

"Greetings," said the red-haired man, glancing at the card. "Misfits, Inc. Cool name."

"Thanks," said Byte. "Yours too."

She crinkled her nose and looked around. The room held a musty scent, a suggestion of old carpeting and old furniture. Against one wall were wooden produce crates, stacked three high to form makeshift bookshelves. Many of the books lining them appeared to be college texts, while others were environmental manifestos bearing titles like *Extinction* and *Earth in the Balance*. Byte resisted the urge to pick one up and flip through it. Posters from the Sierra Club and the World Wildlife Fund covered the walls. One poster, produced by a group called Earth First, depicted a dying Alaska sea otter, its fur blackened with crude oil, its tongue thick and extended as it struggled to breathe.

Byte, a little lost, turned to Jake for help. He stood back

and considered the room with uncertainty, like a person looking over the rims of glasses. The members of Foxfire stared back.

"So…" said Jake, finally leaping in, "you're the radical environmentalists."

"Actually," said Terry, "I prefer the term 'eco-warrior' myself."

The woman in the jungle fatigues—Carol—rose from her chair in a single, crisp movement. She walked to a desk and began tapping at a computer keyboard. Her fingers hammered at the keys, filling the room with a sharp, repetitive *bap! bap! bap!* "You've seen our Web site," she said. "We also produce a quarterly newsletter called 'EarthAlert.'"

"We wanted to do it monthly," added Terry, shrugging an apology, "but we have classes."

Byte moved to the couch and very slowly sat down. She waited a moment for Jake to sit next to her and glared at him when he failed to get the message.

"When we were online," Byte said to the tall man, "you started telling me about something you did at some oil company meeting. What was that all about?"

The man with the hair in his mouth giggled. Terry started to speak, but the woman interrupted, seizing the conversation. "Oh, that," she said. "Actually, you might have read about it in the paper. Texxon was running a processing plant in Oregon, and they were dumping their waste into the Secaugee River."

Byte frowned. "Isn't that illegal?"

88 "Course it is," said the woman. "At first they were fined a couple of times, then the Environmental Protection Agency began running periodic, unannounced inspections of their plant to keep them in line."

"So why didn't they catch them dumping?" asked Jake.

"Texxon was finding out about the inspections in advance. They'd clean up their act in time for the inspectors, then go back to dumping."

"How did they find out the inspection schedule?" Byte asked.

The red-haired young man, Terry, raised his arms toward the ceiling in helplessness. "Ah, she's a babe in the woods," he said. Then he looked at Byte. "Do you know how much money Texxon contributed during the last congressional campaign? Over a quarter million dollars. We figure someone, somewhere, was paying them back by slipping them the information."

"But you couldn't prove that," said Jake.

Terry shrugged. Byte wasn't sure whether the gesture meant *we didn't know for sure* or *we didn't care whether we had proof.*

"So you took matters into your own hands," Byte said.

"Texxon was having this big corporate get-together," said Carol. "The bigwigs flew in from all over the country. So we decided that we should have a representative present as well."

The man with the hair in his mouth giggled again, louder this time.

Terry picked up the story. "So we dressed Paul here in an expensive suit, and we packed a Thermos bottle full of the sludge they were dumping into the river. Then, while a hundred and fifty Texxon shareholders watched a slide show about company growth, we popped the cork, so to speak."

Carol Jablonsky smiled, somehow managing to look angry at the same time. "Paul unscrewed the top of the bottle, set it under his seat, and quietly excused himself from the room. In about three minutes, the place smelled like a flattened skunk. They had to evacuate the room, reschedule the meeting. Took the hotel a whole day to air the place out."

"Didn't you get in trouble?" asked Byte.

"Honey," said Carol, "I'm in law school. We didn't do any monetary damage to the hotel, so a civil suit was out of the question. Texxon might have gotten us on misdemeanor charges—disorderly conduct or some such nonsense—but they couldn't do that without our testifying in court where we got the sludge. That would have brought felony charges against *them*. We had them every which way."

Terry interrupted Carol with a nudge to the shoulder. "Hey," he said, "you're telling our best secrets!"

Byte threw a glance at Jake, wondering what he thought of the conversation, but his face revealed nothing. He had not moved since entering the apartment. His eyes darted from one member of Foxfire to another, measuring each, his thoughts hidden. Now, suddenly intent, he fixed his gaze on Terry Summers. "I'd like an answer to a question," he said. "What's a 'monkey-wrencher'?"

At the sound of the word, Carol spun around and stared at Jake. Terry looked at him, absently scratching at his wispy beard. "Where'd you hear that word?" he asked.

Jake shrugged. "The guys who were chasing us through the woods. One of them yelled it at us."

Terry raised an eyebrow at the mention of the chase, but he reached over into one of the produce crates and withdrew a tattered paperback novel. He tossed it to Jake, who gazed at it a moment before passing it along to Byte.

Byte read the title aloud: *"The Monkey Wrench Gang?"*

"Monkey-wrenching," said Terry, "is guerrilla warfare for environmentalists. Monkey-wrenchers go to where the problem is—where the dam is being built, where the trees are being cut—and they…*attack*. You know, cut the fuel lines of the heavy equipment, pour sugar into gas tanks, slash tires, maybe even put dynamite to a partially completed dam project."

Byte's eyes widened. *Dynamite?* What kind of people was she dealing with here? "But…you don't do *that* kind of stuff…do you?" she asked.

Terry glanced over at Carol Jablonsky, who folded her arms and glared back at him. Apparently, the two had disagreed over this very subject.

"No," said Terry. "We're not that militant. The Texxon incident is about the closest we've come to doing something illegal. Right, Carol?"

"Coward," spat the woman.

"Okaayyy," said Byte. "Let's change the subject. Why don't you guys tell us what you think about this…"

She related what had happened in the woods over the weekend, describing the condition of the birds, the sight of the men, even the echo of the ax handle as it slapped against the man's palm. She then related the events of the following evening. She mentioned the gunshots, but found herself describing in even greater detail the behavior of the forest ranger, the strange arrival of the men at Peter's house, and the confiscation of the bird. The members of Foxfire listened. Carol nodded as though understanding all; Terry murmured long *hmms;* Paul held on to his lock of hair but stopped chewing on it.

"If they were worried about monkey-wrenchers," said Terry, "they must be doing *something* bad to the environment. Something having to do with the stream—or maybe logging."

"Logging shouldn't be killing off kingfishers," said Carol. "They don't nest in trees."

"Besides," asked Byte, "you can't cut down trees in a national forest."

A snorting sound came from Paul, who was still seated on the floor.

"In theory, you can't," said Carol. "In practice, it happens all the time. Congress can auction off logging rights to a company who wants to harvest lumber in a national forest. They don't do it very publicly, though, because it gets people like me *really* upset. We end up putting the information out on the Net, along with the congressman's name, e-mail address, home phone number—anything we can come up with. We've heard some scuttlebutt that some bills have been offered up to stop these auctions, but that the bills never seem to get out of the Resources Committee."

Jake frowned. "I don't get it."

"It works like this," said Carol. "Congress is full of committees that take a first look at bills before sending them out for a vote. The Ways and Means Committee debates each spending bill, the Resources Committee debates each environmental bill, and so on. These committees are like little fiefdoms. If the chair of the committee doesn't like a bill, he or she has the power to tie it up. Congress doesn't even get a chance to vote on it."

"Okay," said Byte, "I think I'm understanding this. You're saying that members of Congress are trying to pass laws to stop these auctions, but this House Resources Committee won't send the bills out so Congress can vote on them."

"Exactly," said Terry.

"Fine, then," said Byte. "We just need to find out who's in charge of the Resources Committee."

No one spoke for a few moments while the members of Foxfire stared at Byte, and Byte began to feel as if she had said something wrong or foolish. Carol Jablonsky exclaimed, "You mean you don't know?"

Byte shook her head.

"Honey, the chairman of the House Resources Committee is *our* congressman—Victor Madison."

Office of Representative Victor Madison
Congressional Office Building
Washington, D.C.

William Benedict had a ritual when the congressman was away.

He stood in the doorway of the congressman's office. A familiar weakness overcame him as he gazed inside, an ache, an envy that made him lean against the door frame and breathe in shallow breaths. He walked to the desk and let his finger skate across the polished surface. The desk was solid mahogany, an antique used almost two centuries ago by John Quincy Adams. William pressed his hand against it and left a spattering of fingerprints on the sheet of glass protecting the desk's surface. Each print was clear and perfect, like the signature at the bottom of one of William's memos to the staff. *This desk is mine,* they seemed to say. William stared at the prints, then wiped at them with the sleeve of his coat.

The chair behind the desk was an old leather wingback with wide flaring sides, thick arms, and brass rivets. Its legs had no casters, only wooden feet carved in the shape of eagles' talons. William stood behind the chair and ran his hand along the top edge.

Now he moved toward the wall of the room and faced the bookshelf. Like the desk, it, too, was mahogany, finished to the color of an old copper coin. It was a lawyer's bookshelf. Glass windows guarded the rows of books. William grasped the wooden knobs on either side of one window, then swung it outward and upward until it was parallel to the floor. From there, the window slid invisibly into the shelf unit along tiny tracks.

So beautiful.

The congressman's law library stood in perfect rows like an ancient encyclopedia. The books were bound—like the desk chair—in burgundy leather, their titles pressed in gold ink. William tipped a volume from the shelf. Once again he felt a swelling inside him, a pride of ownership. He rubbed his thumb across the leather, then he returned the book to the shelf.

The phone jangled. William straightened his tie and cleared his throat before answering it. "Congressman Madison's office."

First silence, then an elderly woman's voice came through the line. "Oh—*William*. May I speak to Victor, please?"

It was Elizabeth Madison, the congressman's wife. William heard the hesitation in her voice and the haughty emphasis on his name. His shoulders stiffened.

"Mrs. Madison," said William, "good morning. I'm afraid the congressman is on the House floor at the moment. He should be returning shortly. May I have him return your call?"

"Please," said the woman. She hung up without another word.

William's fingers squeezed around the phone's handset, tightening until he could almost feel the plastic cracking under the pressure. He willed his muscles to relax, took a deep breath, and placed the phone back in its cradle. On the desk was a message pad bearing the Congressional Seal. William tore off a page and scribbled a note to the congressman. *Mrs. Madison called. 9:07 A.M.* The aide's handwriting was clear and sharp, the points of the *M*s spiking upward like knife blades.

Voices came from the outer office. William heard a chorus of greetings from the secretary and the other aides, then laughter. These were followed by a sound like pebbles skittering down a hill. It was the cracked, gravelly voice of Victor Madison. Moments later, when the congressman reached the inner office, William was standing just inside the door, head up, shoulders straight, hands clasped behind his back like a waiting butler.

"Good morning, Congressman," he said.

"Morning, William."

Congressman Madison walked with a stoop in his shoulders and an unsteady shuffle in his step. As he made his way to his desk, William saw a brief, passing image of the old man falling, breaking a hip. He saw, too, the long convalescence that would follow such an injury—weeks, perhaps months, in bed. He saw the campaign faltering, stumbling to defeat. The last image in this nightmare was the most horrible of all: a new representative, Congresswoman Megan Warwick, sitting at John Quincy Adams's desk.

The chain of thought ran less than half an instant, but in that chain William saw his life, his plans, crumbling.

96   He reached out and touched the congressman's elbow, just to steady the old man a bit.

Madison yanked the elbow away. "I don't need any help, thank you," he said. Then the congressman grasped William's hand in his knotty fingers and gave the hand a squeeze. In response, William felt a surprising rush of affection for the old man.

"Sir," said William, "I've confirmed your flight arrangements. You'll arrive in Bugle Point tomorrow afternoon—in plenty of time to prepare for the debate with Ms. Warwick."

Madison grunted. The pouches of skin beneath his eyes were moist and rimmed with red. He looked exhausted.

Rumors had abounded that the seventy-two-year-old congressman might retire before this campaign—*rumors,* but they had chilled William and sent him into a flurry of action. The words "country" and "duty" came from his lips often, and they appeared most frequently in the messages he left for the congressman. The brass eagle on the congressman's desk bore a new shine. The flag had gone to a dry cleaner. Letters from happy constituents, which the staff usually handled, were left for the congressman to see. When no letters were suitable, William wrote some himself, signing them with phony names.

It was a campaign of subtle manipulation, for in William Benedict's life plan, the congressman must not retire. Not yet.

"And sir," said William, "your wife called. I left the message on your desk."

"Thank you, William," said the congressman, reaching for the phone. "That will be all."

William tipped his head to suggest a bow, then left the office and shut the door behind him. He stood at the file cabinet just outside the inner office and yanked open a drawer. He flipped through some folders, tugging at them here and there, pretending to look at the names. The congressman's voice thrummed through the heavy door.

"No," he was saying, "I won't be gone long. Only three days."

William felt a tingling in his fingertips. The pale skin at his cheeks went warm.

"Dear, I don't need to see a doctor...I'm just a little tired. You know how it is the last few weeks of a campaign.... What?... No, William's handled all the arrangements.... Now, dear, that's hardly fair. He's been with me for years, you know that...."

The congressman's voice grew quiet, and William strained to hear.

"Well, yes, I've given a great deal of thought to what we talked about. But it's just not the right time now. People are counting on me."

The voice became even quieter—a muffled drone, like a distant beehive. William could no longer hear what Madison was saying, but he had heard enough.

His suspicions had been correct. Mrs. Madison had been pressing her husband to retire. She had seen what

William had seen—the occasional unsteadiness in the old man's step, the moisture rimming his eyes, the red veins spiderwebbing across his nose and cheeks, the frequent forgetfulness. The congressman was not up to the rigors of a campaign.

But he would not retire now. William would not allow such a thing.

If Madison were to retire before the election, William's life would be over. Megan Warwick would waltz into Congress with the casual ease of a tourist strolling along the National Mall. William had worked too hard and too long to see his dreams shattered that way. For years he had used his place in this office to make connections with important contributors. Lobbyists had curried favors through him. His signature lay at the bottom of every memorandum. The unspoken word among Washington lobbyists was this: If you want to get something done, you talk to Congressman Madison. And if you want to talk to Madison, you must first go through William Benedict. William needed one more term—two short years—to finish this work. Once he had solidified his position, he would be the obvious choice as the congressman's replacement. He would have shaken all the right hands. He would have all the right money backing him. He would run for Congress.

And he would win.

William nodded to himself. Congressman Madison would not retire, and he would not lose this election. If the old coot died of a heart attack on election day,

William would find a way to prop him up like a ventriloquist's dummy until the congressional session ended.

The door to the office swung open, and Madison stepped out. "Off to my meeting with Senator Hatch," he said. "I'll return after lunch. William, I'll need a practice opponent for the debate. I'm counting on you. The pressroom. Four o'clock."

William nodded.

He watched the congressman shuffle toward the outer door. The old man paused, swaying a bit as he reached for the doorknob. A female aide caught him by the elbow. This time, Madison did not pull away.

William waited a moment before slipping back into the congressman's office. It was not unusual for his duties to bring him here; the other workers would think nothing of the fact that he had shut the door behind him. He reached for the telephone and dialed a number from memory.

"Texxon," said a voice.

"Arthur Maybry, please," said William.

"And who may I say is calling?"

William's thin, hard lips curled into a smile. "Tell him it's Congressman Madison's office."

Arthur Maybry, the president of Texxon, was on the line in thirty seconds. "William," he declared. He paused to wait for information. His tone was somehow both commanding and deferential. It held respect, but also a demand that the respect be returned. It was the way two ancient kings might have spoken to each other—two kings with equal-sized armies. The thrill of it made William's heart pound.

"Just following up, Arthur," said William, "to see that you are satisfied with the progress we've made."

"Quite so," said the executive. "I'm gratified by the effort you've put into our project, William. Monarch is proceeding with its contract ahead of schedule."

"No problems, then?"

Maybry hesitated, but only briefly. "None to speak of. Some kids—high schoolers, really—wandered off the trail and nearly stumbled onto the site, but Monarch's people took care of it. There's no problem."

"Excellent," said William. "Glad to hear it. We aim to please."

He heard Arthur Maybry chuckle as he hung up the phone.

chapter six

nicholas Braddock, Peter's father, sat at his desk and squinted over his daily report. The printing on the form was tiny, dimming here and there to an indecipherable fog of letters. The more he stared, the more blurred the letters became. Nick tossed the form to his desk. He rubbed his eyes and whispered a word under his breath that he would not particularly care to hear his son utter. Then he surrendered to the inevitable: a quick jerk on the handle of his desk drawer revealed a small pair of eyeglasses in cheap, plastic frames. Nick had picked them up a couple of weeks ago from a chain drugstore—reading glasses with magnifying lenses. $9.98. Nick recalled the cardboard advertisement that topped the revolving display—a cartoon of a woman in clothing and hairstyle from the sixties, wearing glasses in huge black plastic frames. Perhaps, Nick thought, the display had sat on the counter about that long.

He put the glasses on, glancing self-consciously at his faint reflection in the office window.

102   Nick worked on the form for several minutes, taking little notice of the other activity around him. As he was finishing, however, the bright light in the office seemed to dim a bit—just enough so that Nick sensed the difference. He raised his eyes from his work.

Agent Polaski was standing in the doorway, blocking the light from the outer office. He was holding a manila folder in his hand. Nick slipped the glasses from his face and set them on the desktop, saying nothing.

Polaski, after a long pause, pointed uncertainly toward the office door. "Going out for some food," he said. Nick found it odd that Polaski would check with him before leaving. The two of them were colleagues of equal experience and rank. Neither was required to ask permission of the other.

"Oh? Fine," said Nick. "Fine." Clearly Polaski had some point in mind. Nick would wait out the conversation until that point was more apparent.

Polaski didn't move. He waved again, and this time Nick became aware that Polaski was gesturing not so much with the hand as with the *folder*.

"This is my report from the other night," Polaski said. He paused to let the statement sink in. "I wanted to turn it in before I left. It'll be by the boss's desk." He took a step away from the door, then looked over his shoulder at Nick. "So if anyone asks, it's in the In basket next to the boss's desk. All right?"

And with that he left.

Nick watched until Polaski was out of sight. *So,* Nick thought, *whatever mess Peter has stepped in, Polaski's not part of it.* The mention of the file, the trouble Polaski went to wave it around and to tell Nick where it would be—Polaski might just as well have read the contents of the file on the six o'clock news. He was going out of his way to invite Nick to read it.

So Nick would do exactly that.

He waited a few moments before fumbling for the glasses on his desk and striding into the office of his superior. On a small shelf unit behind the desk, a stack of file folders lay nested in a wire tray. Nick reached for the top folder in this stack, glanced out the door, and began reading.

According to the report, Polaski didn't know a whole lot more about last Monday night than Nick himself knew. The area in Pine Bluff where the incident occurred was more clearly defined, for Ranger Tummins had provided a map. A remarkably detailed description of Mattie's tennis shoe appeared on one page, and the name, address, home phone number, and social security number of each Misfit appeared on another. A small *hmmph* escaped from Nick as he read. Unlike Peter's description of that night, the report made no mention of rifle fire.

Nick was ready to toss the report aside. It offered few answers and only seemed to add to his list of questions. His hand started to fold the manila cover back over the loose sheets, but something stopped him at the last moment. At the bottom of the page, he saw the name of the person who had filed the complaint. Nick had assumed the complainant against the Misfits was the gentleman who had found Mattie's offending sneaker tangled in the tree root. Nick had figured the guy had told Tummins and that Tummins had called the FBI for backup.

But the report proved Nick Braddock very, very wrong.

At the bottom of the form was a name Nick would not have imagined. Polaski had written it in letters that were larger—and neater—than his usual scrawl. He had wanted to make certain Nick would be able to read them.

The call to the FBI had come from the office of Congressman Victor Madison.

Now why, Nick wondered, *would a U.S. Congressman care about some kids playing around in a national forest?*

And more importantly, *How the devil had he known about the kids to begin with?*

Mattie lay back against the sofa, his arm bent in a crooked circle around his head. On the coffee table in front of him was the handset to the cordless telephone. He stared at it, closed his eyes to think, then stared at it some more. In the last few days, he thought, he had twisted his ankle, lost and regained a tennis shoe, and been shot at by an angry maniac with a rifle. Not to complain, but even by Misfit standards it had not been a good start to the week. And yet, the fear and confusion of the last few days was nothing compared to the inner rumblings he was feeling now.

He was thinking of Caitlyn Shaughnessy. He had thought of her all day at school, had thought of her while visiting with the reporter, had thought of her during the drive home. Now he was waiting for a call from Peter, and he was thinking of her still. Today after third period Caitlyn had taken a fresh stick of chewing gum, one still in its wrapper, and had tucked it deliberately in Mattie's hair. He had pulled it out, saying, "Whadja do that for?"

"Just being generous," Caitlyn had said. "And that is how you like to have your gum served up, isn't it? In the hair, I mean?"

And while Mattie was concocting an answer, Caitlyn had run off to class.

For hours he had replayed that little scene over and over in his mind. Was it an apology of sorts for the other gum incident? A joke at his expense? Had she been…flirting? Mattie couldn't quite figure it out. What if she *had* been flirting with him? What was he supposed to do next? He sat up, his elbows braced against his knees, his head bowed. His eyes focused on the phone.

All I have to do, he told himself, *is pick it up. Punch phone. Dial the number. Let it ring. Listen to her voice when she says hello.* Sure, *starting* a phone conversation with Caitlyn would be simple, but at that point—the moment he imagined her voice reaching his ear—the mental image fell apart. Mattie saw himself stammering. At school he could tear up a playing card and magically restore it, or tell Caitlyn a number she had written down on her palm but hadn't shown him. He could entertain her and at the same time keep himself from thinking about what she might be thinking of him. On the telephone he had nothing but words, nothing but his thoughts and ideas, nothing but his own doubts.

He picked up the receiver, stared down at the open pages of his B.P.H.S. Student Directory, and pressed "phone." The buzz of a dial tone came from the earpiece. Mattie listened to it, pressed a single digit, paused, then scowled in hatred at his own cowardice. His thumb came down hard on the "off" button, and the phone slipped from his fingers and clattered to the tabletop.

He needed more. That was the problem. The way Caitlyn acted—well, it would drive *anyone* crazy. It probably didn't even occur to her that she made him feel like walking over to the living room wall and banging his head against it a few times. But she did.

Yes, before he could tell her what was going on inside him, before he could say, "hey, maybe we could, you know, get together and *do* something," he needed more. He needed a little encouragement. If only she would say, "Call me," and have it mean something other than "let's conjugate those verbs we got for homework—*je suis…tu es…il est…*What time's good for you? I'll jot it down in my Day Runner."

Mattie swiped his sleeve across his mouth and picked up the phone. He would call her. If nothing else—if Caitlyn stammered and made excuses, even if she laughed at him outright—he could at least say he tried. Breathing deeply, he activated the phone and once again began punching in the numbers. The first six went in with ease; however, when it came time to punch the seventh, the one that would actually cause the phone to ring in Caitlyn Shaughnessy's home, he hesitated.

Then he hit the "off" button.

He couldn't do it. He didn't think Caitlyn would laugh. She had never laughed at him before, so he had no real reason to believe she would do so now—but even the thought, the possibility, was terrifying.

Before he could return the phone to its cradle in the kitchen, it jangled in his hand. The sound jarred him. For a moment, he forgot what the ringing meant and what he had to do to make it stop. The phone rang a second time before he caught his breath and activated it.

"Hello?"

"Mattie? It's me," said a voice.

A female voice.

A coldness shot up and down Mattie's spine. His mind was just an instant behind, too late to catch himself and keep his shoulders from shivering involuntarily.

The voice belonged to Byte, not Caitlyn.

"Jake and I just got back. We're at Peter's—and we've found something. Jake's on his way to pick you up. Is that okay?"

Mattie nodded, then mentally kicked himself. *Stupid. She can't see you nodding over the phone.*

"Mattie?"

"Um, yeah—no problem," he said. "I'll see you in a few."

He hit the off button and set the phone back on the coffee table. Though it had not been a long day—at least not yet—he was tired. He stretched out on the couch again and closed his eyes, hoping Jake wouldn't be in too much of a hurry.

He needed a few minutes to think.

Jake was silent during the drive to Peter's—which was not entirely out of character, but Mattie found it strange that his friend refused to answer his questions. Mattie asked anyway, but Jake just shook his head and told Mattie that he would have to wait.

"You have to *see* it," Jake said. He was silent the remainder of the journey, his fingers squeezing the steering wheel.

The silence continued even after they arrived at Peter's. Mr. Braddock stood in the doorway to Peter's bedroom, leaning against the frame with his arms folded. Byte sat on the floor with her back against the wall, and Peter was stretched out across the bed, eyes gazing at the ceiling. He looked over at Mattie, then turned his attention to Byte. Apparently they had been discussing something for some time.

"The answer," Peter was saying, "is to use Rebecca. I'm just not sure what she can do."

"About what?" asked Mattie. He peeled off his jacket and tossed it to the bed, his mind briefly flashing on the reporter. He smiled. He wondered what Rebecca's reaction had been when she tried her pencil sharpener.

Peter nodded toward Byte. "Show him what we've learned."

Byte rose from the floor, and for the first time Mattie noticed that she had been clutching a file folder containing a thin sheaf of papers. She handed the folder to Mattie, her face flat and angry. "Just flip through it," she said. "You'll get the idea."

Mattie glanced at his friends, then slowly opened the file and looked down at the first sheet. He experienced a moment or two of confusion before realizing he was looking at a report Ranger Tummins had filed the night the Misfits had gone back into the woods. Most of the other sheets referred to the same event: a map of Pine Bluff, a somewhat loose description of the Misfits, a logger's words as he described Mattie's missing shoe.

He looked at Mr. Braddock. "This is an FBI file."

Peter walked over, reached over Mattie's shoulders, and flipped through the folder to the last sheet. He pointed his finger at a name on the bottom. Though the name seemed faintly familiar, Mattie did not recognize it.

"Victor Madison?" he asked.

"He's our congressman in Washington," said Peter. He looked at Mattie, pausing to let the weight of his words sink in. "Someone told Madison's office what happened in the woods, and it was Madison's office who sicced the FBI on us." He half-grinned at his father. "No offense."

"None taken," said Mr. Braddock.

"Wait a sec," said Mattie. "I'm confused. Someone called a *congressman* to tell on us for being in the woods?"

Peter nodded.

"Well, what does that *mean?*" asked Mattie.

He looked to the others for an explanation, but none came. Even Mr. Braddock was silent. Peter went back to his bed and sprawled across it, a faint trace of uncertainty on his face as, Mattie supposed, he tried to further analyze the significance of the congressman's involvement. Byte sank into the chair at Peter's desk and leaned back, gently popping open the lid to her laptop computer and snapping it closed again. Jake, scratching his head, reached into his pocket and withdrew his tiny Superball. He sat on the floor and bounced it off the side of Peter's desk, letting it reach nearly to the ceiling and catching it as it arced downward. He repeated the motion again and again. Every time he caught the ball, it slapped against his palm, the sound sharp and rhythmic.

"You think maybe you could STOP DOING THAT?" shot Byte.

Jake, startled, snatched the ball from the air and looked at her. "Sorry," he said.

For a long time the group remained silent. It was Jake who, several moments later, finally broke that silence with a question. "You know what I'm wondering?" he asked. "Maybe this is dumb, but I'm not really all that concerned about the congressman."

"Hmm?" said Peter.

"What scares me," Jake went on, "is the person who *called* this congressman. Someone was able to call Washington, D.C., drag a congressman out of bed in the middle of the night, and have his wishes immediately granted like, I don't know, some kind of foreign leader or something. Doesn't *that* scare the wits out of you? Who has so much power that they can make a U.S. congressman jump through hoops like that?" He put the Superball in his pocket and gazed at the others.

Another long silence ensued. Suddenly Peter—who always seemed to know everything—did something Mattie had never seen before: He looked to his father for help.

"Dad?"

Mr. Braddock's shoulders heaved as he drew in a deep breath. He looked around the room, one finger tapping absently at his chin. Then he smiled and rubbed his thumb against his fingertips, like a man rubbing dollar bills together.

"Money?" asked Peter. "You mean...contributors?"

The question did not hang in the air very long. Mattie watched Peter, fascinated by the way the confused look dropped from his friend's face and an expression of certainty rose to replace it. "Contributors!" Peter shouted. "That's it! People and companies who donate ridiculous sums of money to political campaigns—that's who can wake up a congressman. We need to know who Madison's biggest contributors are."

"Shouldn't be too tough," said Mr. Braddock. "Contributions are public information. Candidates are required to disclose them."

"Byte," said Peter, "can you see if Madison has a Web site?"

Byte was already moving. She popped open her laptop computer, plugged Peter's phone line into the back, and flicked on the power. "That I can do," she said. Mattie followed Peter to her side, and Jake joined them.

"Whoever contacted the congressman's office had to know we were in the woods," said Peter. "It was late, long after the office was closed, and Washington is three time zones away. Even so, someone from the congressman's office called the FBI and demanded that an agent…" He took the file from Mattie's hands and turned to the last page. "…'provide any and all aid requested by the Forestry Service in resolving this matter.' That's a direct quote from the report."

"So," said Byte, "we want to know who could have that kind of pull. Who could just call up someone from a congressman's office and issue an order like that— right?"

She typed "congressman AND victor AND madison" into the search bar provided by her Internet carrier. Seconds later several choices appeared, each in the blue lettering that indicated a link to a Web site. She clicked on one, waited, and a few moments later gestured at the computer screen.

"*Voilà.*"

Mattie saw the cover page to a Web site. At the top of the screen were the words "Victor Madison. U.S. Congress." From a blue field in the upper left-hand corner of the page, a photo of an elderly, smiling man stared out at the viewer. Horizontal stripes of red and white delineated the various areas of the site. The image was meant to look patriotic, Mattie supposed, but the overall effect was a bit heavy-handed and cheesy. "America the Beautiful" played from the computer's stereo speakers.

Byte clicked on one of the red stripes, and the screen image disappeared and turned into a long list. At the top of the list was a brief thank-you:

Congressman Madison would like to thank all the individuals and corporations who gave so generously to his reelection campaign...

The list went on for pages.

"So these are the contributors?" asked Mattie.

"These are the contributors," echoed Mr. Braddock, smirking. "Money—the grease that moves the wheels of government."

"It must be every contributor," said Byte, "or at least every major one. And look—the entries aren't in alphabetical order. They're listed according to how much money the contributor donated."

Jake nodded. "So who's at the top of the list?"

Peter pointed to the screen. The first two names on the list were major media conglomerates; the third—the one Peter indicated—was a company called Texxon.

"Hmm. First see what you can find out about this one," Peter said.

"An oil company?" Mattie asked. "What would they have to do with the forest? Or with kingfishers?"

"Maybe nothing," said Byte, "but let's look at their Web site."

She began a new Web search, and the picture of Congressman Madison slowly faded. A few moments later, an elegant black and gold emblem, the symbol for Texxon Oil, took its place. Byte clicked on a button labeled *The Texxon Family,* and the emblem dissolved. She found herself in another part of the Web site, a lengthy list of what appeared to be names of businesses, other companies Texxon had swallowed up. "I bet this is what we're looking for," she said.

Mattie gazed at the screen.

The names of over a dozen companies appeared. Near the bottom of the list—indicating, perhaps, that Texxon had only recently acquired it—was a company called Monarch Lumber.

"Well, now that's interesting," said Byte.

"Okay, so Texxon owns a lumber company," said Mattie.

"Lumber and forests," Jake said, "okay, they go together, but I still need some help understanding this."

Peter tapped the screen with his forefinger. He frowned, then nodded to himself. "Okay," he said, "suppose this Monarch Lumber Company—a division of Texxon— wants to log in Pine Bluff. The company wouldn't want everyone to know about it, because logging in the national forest would get a lot of environmentalists upset.

So…Monarch's parent company—Texxon—goes to Congressman Madison and says, 'Hey, Vic, ol' buddy ol' pal, remember that fistful of cash I gave you to help with your reelection? Well, I need a little favor. We own this little lumber company now, and we'd like to buy the rights to cut down a few trees in the national forest.'" Peter, excited now, swiped at the clump of hair that continually fell across his eyes. "Next thing you know," he said, "Monarch has its agreement. So if I'm right, they're doing it legally, but they'd like to keep it quiet."

"But what about the birds?" asked Mattie.

Peter shrugged. "That's what I can't figure. Whatever Monarch is doing is somehow affecting the kingfishers. I think that's why the one guy was so angry when he found the dead bird in my backpack. When we went back a second time, we spooked them. They figured we had picked up another bird, so someone at Monarch called Texxon, and Texxon called their pet congressman. Bingo—an hour later the U.S. Forestry Service and the FBI are knocking on my door." He smiled. "They just didn't have a clue that my dad would turn out to be an FBI agent—or that we would have access to this report."

Mattie shook his head. "You're reaching."

"Maybe so," said Peter, "but for now, it's the only explanation that fits all the facts."

Byte closed down her computer. "The only problem is that it doesn't explain what's happening to the birds—or why getting the bird back was so important."

"Maybe the reporter could help us there," offered Jake. "You know, nose around a little."

Mr. Braddock stepped forward. "She might be able to do more than that." Rolled in his fist was today's *Bugle Point Courier*. He tossed it onto Peter's bed, and the paper fell open, revealing the front page. Congressman Victor Madison's face, and the face of his opponent, stared up at the Misfits from a large, grainy photo. The headline read "Candidates to Debate Issues Tomorrow."

"If you want to know what's going on in Pine Bluff," said Mr. Braddock, "maybe your reporter friend should just ask the congressman himself."

"I'll call her tonight," said Peter. He shook his head, and his breath came out of him in a long, tired hiss. "I only wish we had one of the birds. I don't want to go back into those woods to look for another one, though." Here his father glared at him. Peter acknowledged the look with a grin. "And to be honest, I don't think we'd find another at this point—but I sure would like a chance to show one to a vet." He looked at the others. "Oh, well. No use complaining. We'll make do with the information we have."

Mattie stood and tugged on his jacket. "Does that mean we're done?" He caught himself, thinking he had perhaps sounded in too much of a hurry to leave, but the words had just slipped out. The truth was, he was anxious to get back home, where he would once again wrestle with the telephone and thoughts of Caitlyn Shaughnessy.

"Why are you in such a hurry all of a sudden?" asked Byte.

"What?" asked Mattie, trying not to show his impatience. "I'm just starving, that's all. Hey, Jake, you mind if we stop for fast food? I could use a burrito or something. I haven't eaten all day."

At those words, the others stopped what they were doing and stared at him.

"Um...not a problem," said Jake.

"Cool," said Mattie. "Anyone got a couple of bucks?"

Peter raised an eyebrow and shook his head. Mattie looked to Jake, but Jake's eyes narrowed. "Not a chance." He held up his fingers and ticked off a series of Mattie's past debts. "Five bucks for a trick deck of cards at the magic shop. Ten for a 'Super-Heroes of the AC Universe' T-shirt. Another five for that antique tube radio at the pawn shop."

Mattie put on his widest grin and turned to Byte. "Byte," he said, "you know I love you."

Byte rolled her eyes and reached for her fanny pack. Mattie watched as she felt around inside it, shuffling items here and there. She tugged out a small wallet, but found only some change inside. Finally she took the entire pack and turned it upside down, dumping its contents onto Peter's desk. She rummaged through everything and found three singles folded into a tight, flat wad. Just as Mattie reached for the bills, Byte's eyes turned back to the desktop and to her pile of scattered belongings. Her hand hovered in the air, trembling. The bills slipped from her fingers and fell to the floor.

"Byte?" said Peter.

118 She reached down and pinched a tiny object between her thumb and forefinger, raising it to the light.

It was a feather—small, white, and flecked here and there with gray.

Peter, Jake, Mattie, and Mr. Braddock gathered around Byte and stared at the feather. She twirled it between her fingers, letting it catch the light from Peter's desk lamp.

"It must have been left over from when the Baggie broke the other night," she said quietly. Her face looked yellow in the lamp's harsh light. "Do you think we can use this? I mean, do you think someone could tell what's happening to the birds just from a single feather?"

"Not likely," said Peter. "It's—it's been in your pack for a full day," he said, speaking slowly, his eyes locked on the feather—and, perhaps, on the possibilities it presented. "It's probably touched everything in there. Grimy coins. Kleenex tissue. Your, um…Kermit the Frog key chain. I'm sure it's useless as a sample."

"You're probably right," said Jake. It seemed for a moment that the matter was settled. The feather was too small, too contaminated to be of value.

"So," Jake added, "who's going to check the Yellow Pages for a vet?"

"I will," said Mattie.

"Right." Peter frowned. "No, wait," he said. "Not a vet. We need a lab, I think. Some place where this feather can be analyzed."

"We could check with Decker," Byte offered.

Peter offered a vague nod. He seemed hypnotized by the feather. "Right. We'll do that tomorrow."

Byte was silent. The feather remained in her hand, still twirling. And though it was faint, Mattie thought he saw a hint of triumph flicker across her face.

Bugle Point Police Department
Wednesday afternoon

The following day Peter, Byte, Jake, and Mattie found Lieutenant Marvin Decker sitting at his desk, surrounded by several bottles of brightly-colored, syrupy liquids and foil packs containing capsules filled with tiny, rainbow-colored grains. Decker's eyes were bloodshot, his nose red and swollen. As the Misfits approached, he grabbed a tissue and honked into it. Peter glanced down and took a quick inventory of the items on the detective's desk.

"Cold, Lieutenant?"

Decker waved away the question. "Nah, I'm fine." He coughed once. "Last night I sneezed, and my wife ran out and bought the entire pharmacy." He punched two capsules through the package's foil backing and tossed them into his mouth, swallowing them with gulp of what appeared to be hot lemon water. Then he glared at each of the Misfits, as if daring them to say another word about his condition. "What do you need?"

The question was straightforward, and Peter took it to be Decker's best compliment. The Misfits had helped Decker on a few cases in the past, and the fact that he had asked them so quickly what they needed, without spending time on preliminaries, meant they had earned his respect.

Byte reached into her pack and took out a sandwich bag containing the feather. "We need to learn everything we can about this," she said. "Can you help us?"

Decker's natural frown seemed to deepen, if that were possible. Peter worried for a moment that the detective would start asking a lot of questions. But this time they were in luck. Decker seemed more interested in getting rid of them than finding out about the feather. He hauled himself from his chair and gestured for Peter, Byte, Jake, and Mattie to follow him. He led them down a long hall, shuffling the entire way and occasionally dabbing at his nose with a handkerchief. The hallway made a sudden cut to the right and came to a dead end at a set of double doors. A sign on one door said Laboratory, and on a line below that, Marco Weese, Forensics.

Decker placed his palm against the door to push it open, then stopped suddenly. From behind, Peter saw the detective raise one hand in the air as though he had just remembered something. He patted the door lightly and turned to face the Misfits.

"Listen," he said in an unnaturally deep and froglike voice. He coughed again. "I'll let you in here, but you gotta promise me you won't, you know, *do* anything."

None of the Misfits spoke. Peter tried to imagine what exactly the lieutenant was afraid they might do, but nothing occurred to him.

"Sir?" said Jake.

"Oh, nothing personal," said Decker. "It's just that—"
He glanced at the door. "Well, the guy who runs the lab
is kind of, you might say, *protective* of his work space.
You know what I mean? So just, I don't know, just don't
do anything—if you get my drift."

With that, he faced the door again and pushed it open.
As they filed into the lab, Mattie tapped on Peter's shoulder. "Do *you* get his drift?" Mattie whispered. Peter
shook his head.

Peter had a very clear image in his mind of what a
police lab should look like, and except for some minor
differences, this lab matched the image perfectly. The
light in the laboratory was staggeringly bright. A stainless steel counter ran along the length of three of the
lab's four walls, broken in two places by wide, stainless
steel sinks. In a quick glance, Peter saw no fewer than
three microscopes, two autoclaves, and several metallic
stands that were connected, with latex surgical tubing, to
nozzles rising from the countertop. *Bunsen burners.*
Against the fourth wall was a huge, modular shelf unit
holding dozens of bottles of chemicals.

The forensic scientist who ran the lab turned to face
the Misfits. He was approximately Peter's height, but
darker in complexion and thin as a whippet. He wore
huge glasses with tortoise-shell frames. They rode
loosely on his nose, and when he turned suddenly they
pitched forward, falling against his chest and dangling
by yellow surgical tubing. He grabbed them with

nervous hands and placed them back onto his face. He studied the Misfits, his eyes focusing first on one, then on another, until Peter began feeling a little like a specimen himself. A photo ID badge hung from the pocket of the man's lab coat. It identified him as Marco Weese, Forensic Scientist.

"Yes?" said the scientist. His voice was sharp, Peter thought, and had a faintly nasal quality that grated on the ears.

"Marco," said Decker, "these are friends of mine. I told them that, if you had a little time, you might help them with some lab work." He coughed again, the sound rumbling from deep within his chest.

"Better take care of that cold," said the scientist.

"I don't *have* a cold," snapped Decker. He turned on his heels and pushed open the door leading to the hallway. An instant later he was gone, his presence marked only by the fading click of his footsteps as he strode, quite firmly, down the hall. Peter thought he could hear the man muttering.

"Hmm," Weese muttered, "it's wonderful to know that my colleagues think I have so little to do." His eyes again darted from one Misfit to another, searching for a leader. "Well? What do you want?"

Byte took half a step forward, her shoulders hunched slightly. She held out the bag containing the feather. "We were wondering," she said, "if you could take a look at this. It came from a dead bird, and we'd like to know what killed it."

The scientist snorted. "Hmmph. Not asking much." He took the bag and held it up to a lamp that shone from within a large, conical reflector in the ceiling. The scientist's eyes squinted from behind his huge glasses. "I'm a bit of a birder myself," he said, his voice trailing off, softening somewhat. "Do you know the species?"

"Belted kingfisher," said Jake.

Mattie had made his way around the lab, gazing at all the expensive equipment. He put his pinky finger into one of the holes of an autoclave and gave the unit a little spin.

"Don't do that again," snapped Weese, without so much as looking in Mattie's direction. Instead, the scientist fixed his gaze on Jake, then on the feather. His eyebrow arched with doubt. "Belted kingfisher, you say? Really? Hmm…" He turned the bag so that it caught the light better, studying the feather for several long seconds. Then he let the bag fall to the countertop.

"Come back in two hours."

Two hours later, they found Marco Weese pretty much where they had left him, standing beneath a reflector that threw down an intense, white cone of light onto a lab table. He was still holding the plastic bag containing the feather, still gazing at it. When the Misfits entered, he turned to face them, a smile on his face that flickered briefly before vanishing behind another look that Byte could not interpret.

Perhaps sensing that she was driving force behind this investigation, Weese looked first at Byte. "You know," he said, "I find this very fascinating."

Jake pulled his Superball from his jacket pocket let it drop from his fingers. It struck the linoleum floor and bounced back up like a rocket, vanishing into his palm. The scientist glared, but said nothing. Jake pursed his lips and put the ball away.

"So," Jake said, "can you tell us what killed it?"

Weese's lips stretched into a thin line, but Byte thought the grin was hiding a feeling other than joy. She suddenly suspected that the man did indeed have the answer—and moreover, that his discovery had deeply disturbed him.

"I'm quite proud of this," Weese said, his voice oddly flat for someone expressing pride.

He led the Misfits to a section of stainless steel counter. On the counter stood a microscope and several petri dishes, each dish filled with a lightly colored fluid.

"The feather was smeared with fish oil and bits of fish tissue," the scientist went on.

Peter, who was always curious about the scientific side of police investigations, raised his hand. "How did you determine that?" he asked.

The scientist stared at him. "I *sniffed* it."

Peter nodded, silent, his face flushing bright red.

"I also did a little chemical analysis," Weese said. "Something odd came up. The…fish matter…smeared on the feather contained minute traces of some non-organic chemicals."

"Which means what?" asked Jake.

"I couldn't tell you exactly," said the scientist, "except to say that, whatever these chemicals are, they definitely did not arrive naturally. You don't find man-made chemicals in a fish unless someone put them there."

"And this chemical killed the bird?" asked Peter.

Weese nodded once, slowly. "It's quite possible."

Byte felt her stomach contract. The space it left grew very cold, and she had to force herself to breathe steadily for a moment or two before she could respond. "So what are you saying?" she asked. "What's happening out there?"

Weese looked at her. "I'd need an actual sample of the chemical to tell you more."

Peter nodded to himself, and Byte could almost see the new information slowly seeping into his understanding of the case. "Is there a phone I can use?" he asked. He looked at the others. "I want to call that reporter."

The scientist pointed to the other side of the lab. "There," he said. "Dial nine to get out."

Byte, trembling slightly, half remembered a small, castered desk chair that lay nearby. Her hand drifted behind her until she felt the chair's padded, metal back. She drew the chair to her and slid into it, her arms circling her upper body. Was it possible? Some man-made chemical was killing the birds? She had to know for sure. Scrabbling through the nylon bag containing her laptop, she found one of the Misfits' business cards and wrote her e-mail address on the reverse side. She then handed the card to Weese.

"I'll leave the feather with you," she said. "If you learn anything else, please let me know."

A moment or two later Peter returned. "I caught her."

"What did she say?" asked Mattie.

Peter smiled. "She thought the lead we have was very interesting. She also mentioned that the press conference with the two congressional candidates is at four o'clock tomorrow." He looked at the others, his smile taking on a sly and somewhat satisfied edge. "And she asked if we were doing anything tomorrow afternoon."

chapter
seven

Pine Bluff Woods

Jerry Vitale sat in his office and drew his hand back and forth across his cheek, feeling the scrape of five days' growth of beard. Nearby, a thirteen-inch television, fed by a small satellite dish, hummed and flickered through an episode of Oprah. Jerry's daughter, who was twenty-five years old and working for him now full-time, threw a quick glance at the screen when Oprah circled her arm around the shoulders of a weeping guest.

Jerry ran his palm across his beard again and said, "Karen, honey, would you send Zach in for me, please?"

Karen turned off the set and headed for the door, snatching a red jelly bean from the jar on Jerry's desk as she passed.

"And then would you excuse us for a few minutes?"

She paused, her face studying his for a moment. Then she nodded once and left.

Jerry leaned back in his chair and gazed about the room. The mobile office was a blessing, he thought. The access to television gave the men something to do at night, when they had nowhere to go and it was too dark to work. A second satellite dish provided telephone communications. Indeed, Jerry felt a touch of the miraculous in every gadget in this building—a building that was little more than a trailer, really. From here he could manage every facet of his business, from sending faxes and e-mail to computing the exact value in board feet of a given tree. He could call in the helicopter, or order a pizza. Thank heavens Karen was here to help out with the technical stuff, though.

He laughed softly to himself. He could do so much at the touch of a few buttons. It seemed he could control everything—except Zachary Morgan's temper. *No matter how modern the world gets,* he thought, *some things never change.*

A few minutes later, Zach pushed open the flimsy door to the trailer and stepped inside. His boots thudded heavily against the light floor, vibrating the plastic caddy of Post-it Notes on Jerry's desk. Jerry placed his hand on the caddy, steadying it.

Zach stood above him, pine scent permeating his skin and clothes, sweat glistening on his face and darkening the armpits of his shirt.

"Yeah?" he said.

Jerry rubbed his palm against his beard again and gestured to the chair facing his desk. Zach reached for the chair, swung it around, and straddled it.

Zachary Morgan was much taller than Jerry—less muscular, but harder and leaner. Jerry had a noticeable belly on him and was thicker and stronger in the upper body. Jerry occasionally wondered if Zach's new lean-ness—the razorlike edges of his cheekbones and jaw-line—weren't partly connected to what had happened to Tim Breen three years ago. Since the accident—though "accident" was hardly what the men would call it—Zach had worked harder, spoken less, eaten less. In the past few years, the Zach Jerry once knew had burned away like so much dry kindling.

"It's about the other night," said Jerry. "I've been want-ing to talk to you about it. Thought this was a good time."

After a moment's pause, Zach said, "You mean the monkey-wrenchers."

"We don't *know* that they were monkey-wrenchers!" The words came out of Jerry louder than he had intended. Zach had been stupid, bringing the gun, shooting at those kids, but he was still Jerry's partner. Zach, like Jerry, was from the old school. Protect yourself first. Protect your men.

Zach stared at the floor and shook his head. "You're too trusting."

"I saw them," said Jerry. "They were just kids."

Zach did not raise his voice. Instead, he spoke in a growl-like whisper, which carried even more threat than a shout would have. "They were monkey-wrenchers. You want to believe they were just kids? Just out for a little Sunday hike? Fine, go ahead. But they were way off the trail, and one of them had picked up a dead bird."

"Doesn't mean anything," said Jerry, but he said it qui-etly, his eyes cast downward, because he knew even as he said it he was wrong. Those kids, the dead bird—it all meant *something.* Monkey-wrenchers? Possibly. But unlike Zach, Jerry needed to know more before he picked up a gun. "This is too important," he said. "Too much can go wrong. I don't want it to be like it was before—the protests, the news cameras, some wacko setting up a tent in a tree."

"There's only one way to deal with monkey-wrenchers," said Zach. "If you don't keep them scared, they'll come back. It'll happen again—*just like before.*"

Jerry shook his head. His fingers nervously played with the desk caddy. "I'm not ready to believe that. You were wrong the other night. You were out of control. Someone might have gotten hurt."

Zach's hand came down on the desktop. Before Jerry could react, before he could even think, Zach picked up the caddy of Post-its and hurled it against the wall. The plastic cracked, sending up a cloud of canary-colored bits of paper that fluttered to the floor. "Someone *has* gotten hurt! You were trusting then! You wouldn't listen to me then, and Tim Breen bled to death—all because of a monkey-wrencher. I'm telling you now, Jerry, if you don't listen to me, there'll be more blood—and this time around it'll be your fault."

Jerry braced his hands against the desk and pushed his chair away from it. He glared at Zach, silent. If one of the other men had spoken to him this way, Jerry might have fired him—or hit him. But this was Zach, and Zach deserved a fair hearing—even when he was wrong. Jerry rose and took a few steps toward the window, staring out at the men and the heavy equipment. He thought of the accident. He couldn't help it. Zach's words had brought him there. In an instant he was standing again in Las Cruzas, and Tim Breen was once more a smiling, muscular nineteen year old.

Then Jerry saw the accident all over again, in that deadly slow motion that only the imagination can produce. He heard the metallic grinding, saw the broken chain spiraling outward, watched it lash Tim's neck and chest.

Now, three years after the fact, Jerry squeezed his eyes shut, trying to push the memory out.

Monkey-wrenchers. What if it were true? Jerry had learned by the blood of one of his own men not to take chances, but still…

Jerry would hate to make the same mistakes he had made before—to be too naïve, too trusting, too willing to accept that the other side had honest intentions. At the same time, he worried over the state of his own soul if he went Zach's way: too quick to anger, too willing to reach for the gun. If he and Zach were wrong, and an innocent hiker died simply because he and Zach no longer *believed* in innocence, Jerry would feel he had lost everything.

No, he insisted to himself. Jerry would find a way to protect the men, the equipment, and the job without falling prey to the paranoia he saw in Zach.

"We're not going to get crazy with this," he said. "Not until we're sure those kids are monkey-wrenchers."

"Well, I'll tell you something," said Zach. He spoke in the same low growl he had used a few moments ago, leaving Jerry with little doubt as to what he was going to say. "I'm sure enough already. If I see them around here again, Jerry, I'll get rid of them for good. And that's a promise."

Jerry did not reply. He continued staring out the window as Zach's heavy bootfalls thudded across the floor and down the metal steps outside. Jerry's only thought as Zach left was that if he were certain…if he were dead certain those kids *were* monkey-wrenchers, Zach would not stand alone. Jerry would stand beside him, and he would fight Zach for the chance to shoot first.

"Congressman! Congressman!" The words seemed to trip over themselves, cascading in different rhythms, rising and falling in pitch as dozens of reporters vied for attention. "Congressman, a question please…"

Peter resisted the urge to clamp his hands down over his ears. He hated crowds. In small groups, his knack for observation really shone. He could catch the light sound of footsteps tapping behind him; he would mentally log the emblem on a stranger's T-shirt, the shape of a girl's earrings, the scar on a bus driver's knuckle. In crowds this thick, however, where people thronged around him like mall shoppers at Christmas, Peter's senses overloaded. A camera team from the network news station shone bright spotlights onto the stage where the two candidates stood.

Photographers from several newspapers shot frame after frame of film, their flashes flickering like strobe lights in Peter's eyes. Trying to observe people here was like trying to do quiet deduction in a disco.

Congressman Madison, though stooped and clearly frail, was still somehow commanding with that great shock of white hair and those piercing blue eyes. The skin below the eyes was drooping. Madison looked like an aging general weary of battles.

In contrast, the congressman's opponent—Megan Warwick, a former mayor of Bugle Point—stood poised and erect at her podium, providing a youthful counterpoint to the congressman's hesitant step.

Both candidates stood on a large, carpeted platform that had been erected especially for the press conference. The questioning would take place here, in the Grand Meeting Room of the Bugle Point Regency Inn, perhaps the most luxurious hotel in the city. Peter noted the black marble tile on the floor, the gold leaf tracing through the wallpaper, the brass highlights on the support pillars. To add a bit of color, the event planners had placed potted trees and hanging plants throughout the room.

Peter felt Jake's finger tapping him on the shoulder. "So," said Jake, "where's your reporter?"

"Yeah," said Byte, shivering a little. "I feel a little weird just standing here. Do you have any idea what we're supposed to be doing?"

Peter frowned. "Let's see if we can find out." He looked at Mattie, who, without an instant's hesitation, stepped up onto the edge of a heavy pot in which a sizeable rubber tree grew. Mattie held on to the trunk of the tree for balance and peered out over the throng of reporters. After several long moments passed, he pointed toward the double wooden doors in the back of the room. "I think she just came in," he said.

Mattie hopped off the plant container and slipped into the crowd, weaving his way through the throng of people. For an instant he was a little more than a flash of yellow—the color of his T-shirt—and then he vanished completely. While he was gone, none of the Misfits spoke. The general understanding was that he would not be gone very long.

A few moments later, a skinny arm wriggled out from between the two reporters standing nearest to Peter. Both reporters, surprised, arched their backs a little and separated. Mattie squeezed his way between them, saying, "Excuse me…coming through…excuse me…" His left hand trailed behind him, and as he drew it from between the two men, Rebecca Kaidanov—blinking and out of breath—came with it.

Mattie put on a little show for his friends, blowing on his fingernails nonchalantly then polishing them against his shirt. "Miss me?" he asked.

The reporter surveyed the room, blinking. She shook her head. "I was with you the whole time," she said, "and I still can't figure out how you got us here."

She turned toward Peter and smiled, extending her hand. "Hi. Sorry I'm late. You can't imagine how hard it is to get past the security here when you have a Russian accent."

Peter smiled. "Not a problem. Byte, Jake, meet Rebecca Kaidanov." They exchanged introductions, and Peter turned his attention back to the platform and the two candidates.

"So, Rebecca," he said, "what's the next step?"

The reporter reached into her satchel, withdrawing a palm-sized spiral notebook and a microcassette recorder. "We listen, and I take notes," she said. "And at the right time, I ask questions." She placed a fresh cassette into the recorder and pressed the record button, catching the congressman's voice as he replied to the first of the afternoon's questions.

"The press conference will last about forty-five minutes," whispered Rebecca. "At five o'clock, the candidates will move off with their respective campaign teams, eat a quick dinner, and begin what will most likely be rigorous practice sessions in preparation for the debate, which is scheduled for later this evening."

Congressman Madison droned on about one issue after another, his voice starting off strong and rich, but faltering as the conference wore on. Megan Warwick, on the other hand, seemed to grow stronger and more vibrant with every question.

"Well, now we know why Madison's having such a hard time with this campaign," whispered Byte. "Check out his competition."

Jake grinned. "You're only saying that because it's a woman."

When he heard a sudden burst of breath explode from Jake, Peter sighed. He had sensed it coming: Byte had thrown an elbow into Jake's diaphragm.

As the five o'clock hour approached, the pace of the questioning slowed. Reporters had covered most of the major issues, and only less substantial matters remained. The candidates began speaking in lofty language of flag and family, quoting Lincoln and Jefferson and, Peter thought, not really saying much of anything.

"What exactly are we doing, anyway?" asked Mattie.

Rebecca held her recorder up a little higher. "Waiting for a lull," she whispered. "And I think it's come." She began waving her arm for attention. "Congressman Madison! Congressman! A question…"

Her voice rang out just as the others trailed off. It filled the room, and the candidate turned toward it.

"Yes?"

"Congressman," said Rebecca, "Rebecca Kaidanov of the *Courier*. Has your office arranged for the auctioning of logging rights in the national forest? And if so, why is the logging being kept a secret?"

Peter saw the congressman's shoulders lurch backward slightly, as though the question had struck him in the chest. As Madison opened his mouth to speak, a faint breath sounded through the microphone. Then the man sagged a bit. Pausing to lick his lips, he croaked, "Logging? A secret?" His voice barely carried, even through the microphone. As though to steady himself against falling, he gripped the edge of the podium. The momentary pause permitted the explosion that followed.

"Congressman," shouted a reporter. "What about this? Shouldn't voters be allowed to decide whether or not to allow logging in the national forest?"

"Is this a change in your environmental policies?" shouted another.

"Are you in favor of clear-cutting?"

The questions piled one on top of another, like players in a rugby game. The reporters' voices clamored. Arms waved in the air, demanding attention. Dozens of camera flashes began firing, further startling the congressman and almost physically pushing him backward. He fell away from the podium, stumbled, and in an instant an aide stepped up behind him, grabbing his elbow. Peter watched, frowning. The aide, a tall man in a navy blue suit, white shirt, red tie, and ivy-league haircut, bent down to the microphone and flashed a warm smile. "That will be all," he said. "Thank you for coming." He waved to the reporters, who were still shouting questions, and gently led the old man away.

In the raucous environment of the room, few were paying attention to the aide as he guided the congressman from the platform. Most were tossing questions at Megan Warwick. Some eyed Rebecca, perhaps in envy of the circus she'd caused by her question.

Peter, however, would not take his eyes off the man in the suit. He had learned long ago from his father that

138 people revealed far more about themselves when they weren't aware they were being watched. As Congressman Madison headed toward a side exit, surrounded by his staff and by police, the aide did something Peter did not expect. He stepped away from the crowd and looked back toward the crowd of reporters. His eyes scanned the room, searching—it seemed to Peter—until they fell on Rebecca Kaidanov. For the longest time the man seemed to stare at the reporter, measuring her, and then he glanced at each of the Misfits.

A moment later, he and the rest of the congressman's staff disappeared.

Frowning, Peter turned his attention from the abandoned podium to the herd of reporters surrounding the somewhat startled Megan Warwick. She attempted to field each question, but she could only stammer out the answers, searching vainly for the right words, her eyes occasionally flickering toward the empty podium beside her.

"Not to sound dumb," murmured Jake, "but what just happened?"

Rebecca grinned. "I don't have a clue," she said, "but I *loved* it."

William Benedict gripped the congressman's elbow just long enough to pass the old man along to one of the other aides. "Watch him," he whispered. "We can't have him falling."

"I heard that, William," the congressman bellowed. "You don't have to treat me like a child!"

William ignored the comment. He stepped aside and looked back out over the room of reporters, searching for a face.

There…

His eyes fell on a young woman with coarse dark hair. She was scribbling into a small, wire-bound notepad; the hint of satisfaction playing across her face made William's insides boil. *Kaidanov. Rebecca Kaidanov, she had said. With the* Courier. He shook his head, angry with himself. *A local reporter, too.* A part of him had expected this. William's first axiom of politics: *It does not matter how cleverly you hide something; the press will find it.* The trick was in planning, in readying a quick response when the news hit. William was furious with himself because he had forgotten this simple truth. He had hidden his actions so well, he believed the press could not possibly uncover them, and yet somehow this woman had. A *local* reporter! If William had been a candidate for Congress, and one of his own aides had behaved so stupidly, he would have fired the fool on the spot. Now William himself was the fool.

Moving back up the hall, William turned toward the meeting room instead of toward the elevator that would have taken him to Madison's suite. The others could take care of the old man. William had to attend to business. He scanned the crowd until he once again located the reporter—Kaidanov; he must remember that name.

Watching her—noting her youth, her apparent inexperience—William pondered the biggest question of all: *How had she gotten the story? Who was her source? Someone connected with the congressman's office? Someone at Monarch? At Texxon?*

She was chatting, laughing with the four teenagers who gathered around her. Then, in a move that William Benedict found particularly annoying, she strode off toward the bank of phones in the lobby—undoubtedly to phone her story in to her paper. William could only imagine tomorrow's headlines.

One of the teenagers—a boy, perhaps sixteen, with dark hair and glasses—glanced back at William. The two locked eyes for a moment, and it seemed to William that the boy was measuring him, studying him the way a boxer might study a film of his next opponent. But that was ridiculous. The boy would not even have noticed William, except for that brief moment when William had spoken into the microphone. His thoughts were bordering on paranoia now.

Then it struck him. *Teenagers. High schoolers.* It seemed unlikely—even impossible—that these were the ones who had approached Monarch's site a few days ago, but William had long ago learned that the impossible sometimes crept up on you and bit you on the behind.

He slowly flipped down the mouthpiece to his cell phone and punched in a series of numbers on the keypad with the ball of his thumb. As he did, he stepped back into the hallway out of view.

The phone rang ten, eleven times before someone answered, but that was to be expected.

Pine Bluff Woods

Zachary Morgan raised his arms into the air, signaling the approaching chopper. He wore a tight-fitting pair of leather work gloves that had, over the years, stiffened with dirt, sweat, and the sap of countless trees. In these gloves he felt a warmth, a comfort and familiarity that even the most expensive pair of new gloves could not have given him. He wore them everywhere except to eat, bathe, and sleep.

He waved one arm in a broad circular motion, guiding in the chopper. His other hand rested against the trunk of a fallen Douglas fir, cleaned of its branches by chainsaws. As the helicopter drew closer, it slowed, hovering over the tree like a praying mantis over a beetle. Cables dropped from the chopper's fore and aft ends. Zach, along with another logger, quickly attached the cables to either end of the tree trunk. The helicopter's rotors growled in his ears and kicked dust in his face as he worked. Zach quickly secured the cable and stepped away, at the same time shielding his eyes and checking to see that the other man had moved to safety as well. When Zach saw that he had—and saw the man signaling that his cable, too, was secure—he gazed up again at the helicopter and motioned it off. *All clear, take it away.*

Zach could just make out the helicopter pilot nodding, indicating that he understood.

The chopper rose a few inches, and the cables grew taut. At this point the chopper held fast in the sky, the cables straining, and Zach could almost see them tremble. Slowly, the helicopter began to rise, taking the tree with it. It hovered in the air, arced into a slow turn, then headed in the direction of the logging road, where the giant hauler—an eighteen-wheel flatbed truck—waited.

Only when the chopper had left, the roar of its engines finally fading, could Zach hear what was going on around him. A voice called his name several times, and when he turned toward the sound, he saw one of the other men—the old-timer named Eli—holding the satellite phone in the air and waving it at him. Zach walked over and took the phone from Eli's hand, placing it to his ear. "Yeah?"

"Can you talk?"

Zach recognized the voice immediately. It was Benedict, from the congressman's office. Zach glanced at Eli and walked away, taking the phone with him. "I can now," he said.

"Have you been watching CNN?"

Zach, sweat dripping off his nose and the tip of his chin, almost laughed. "You've got to be kidding."

"We have a little problem. A reporter's gotten a whiff of what we're doing, which means we have a leak somewhere. Are you sure you can you trust your men?"

"I trust *all* my men," said Zach. "Look somewhere else for your leak." He pointed at a man who had just yanked the starter pull on his chainsaw, then indicated the tree the man was clearly set to begin cutting. A slash of red paint, left by the Forestry Service, marked the tree. The tree was old growth—forbidden. Another concession to the monkey-wrenchers and environmental wackos. Zach pointed instead to a different tree. *Not that one,* he mouthed. *This one.* The man nodded.

Benedict, Zach noted, had not spoken for a moment. When he finally did speak, his voice grew quieter and somehow deeper. "I thought as much," he said. "I have another question. The other day you mentioned that some teenagers had wandered off the trail. Were there four of them? And was one of them a dark-haired, skinny kid wearing glasses?"

Astounded by the mention of the four monkey-wrenchers, Zach stopped walking. "Yeah, that sounds like the leader, the kid who had the bird wrapped up in his pack."

Benedict paused. "That's very interesting. I think I may have solved the problem of our leak. Those teenagers— your monkey-wrenchers—are working with a reporter. It may be necessary to throw a scare into her."

Zach shot nervous glances at the men working around him, as if they might have heard. Many of them would no doubt disapprove of what he was doing, had they known. Certainly Jerry would disapprove, but Jerry had always been a bit too trusting when it came these matters.

"Tell me what you have in mind," said Zach.

"She's young, inexperienced. It shouldn't take much to drive her off the story."

Benedict hadn't hesitated before answering, and Zach instantly disliked him for it. The man had brought up the idea of violence—necessary violence, but violence nonetheless—without so much as a thought about what he was asking. Or the consequences. Zach had no respect for men like this, men with Ivy League educations who thought the universe orbited around them. This Benedict guy was willing to do violence to a reporter merely because he wanted something, and the reporter was in his way. Zach, too, was willing to do violence if necessary, but only because he saw this reporter as a genuine threat—to himself, to his life, to his living. She was on the side of the monkey-wrenchers, and monkey-wrenchers were murderers, plain and simple. To save yourself, you attacked them first. And there was nothing morally wrong in that.

"I'll let you decide what will work," said Benedict, "but you'll have to act soon—before she uncovers anything else."

Zach had a greater concern than the reporter. "What about the monkey-wrenchers?"

"The kids?" Benedict paused. "I hadn't really considered them. Do whatever you think is necessary. I'll call you back in an hour with the reporter's name, home address, phone number, and the make, model, and license number of her car."

"You can do that?"

Zach heard a chuckle, then a dial tone.

The lumberman shut down the satellite phone, walking the few paces to return it to its cradle. It was good that it was almost time for his break. He had something to do.

Zach stepped into the bed of a panel truck and moved aside a sheet of burlap, uncovering a two-gallon metallic container with a screw-down chrome spout. The men were busy, paying little attention to him, so Zach slipped behind the truck and trudged off into the woods, lugging this container with him.

After a few minutes of walking, he found the trail. He followed it for a couple of hundred yards before stepping back into the woods. At the higher elevations, last winter's snows were melting and trickling down the mountain in rivulets. Zach could hear, just ahead, the rushing water of the swollen stream. He walked toward the sound, hearing it grow louder as he approached. His shoulder ached from the weight of the container, and he shifted it to his other hand.

When he finally stood at the edge of the stream, he could see the little fish darting about in the water. Zach studied them a moment, his breath leaving him in a sigh. He hoisted the can, getting a better grip on it, then overturned it. A light green liquid poured from the can into the water. Zach let perhaps a gallon of the fluid flow out before righting the can and setting it down in the moist soil. Strangely, as he watched the liquid swirl into the stream water, an image of Jerry came to his mind. Zach had to push the image out.

He sat at the water's edge for several minutes, his eyes closed and his head lowered.

chapter eight

Thursday

mattie found the others waiting for him at their customary spot. On a rainy day it was a table in the far corner of the cafeteria. On a day like today, when the sun was bright and the spring air was cool, it was a pair of concrete benches in the grassy area just off the quad.

Mattie walked up to his friends with his head slightly bowed. He had never before been so late to one of their meetings. Jake crumpled his hamburger wrapper and, without taking his eyes off Mattie, tossed it so that it landed in a nearby trash can. Peter sat on a bench, gazing through the clump of hair that was always falling across his eyes. Byte crinkled her nose to set her wire-framed granny glasses straight. Of the three, only she was smiling, no doubt having guessed where Mattie had been.

"Hi," said Mattie, "sorry I'm late."

Peter tossed his hair out of his eyes with a flick of his head. "I thought it might be a good time for us to talk about where we are. You know, take a look at everything we've learned, maybe try to put some of the pieces together."

"Three minutes till the bell rings," said Jake.

"We don't really have time then, do we?" asked Mattie, biting his lip. He hadn't quite gotten up the nerve yet to look his friends in the eye.

"We can meet this evening," suggested Byte. "We'll be able to do more then, anyway—right?"

Jake had been twirling his Superball between his fingers. He bounced it hard against the concrete, and it soared in a tall, straight line over his head. A moment later it came down, smacking into his palm. "Works for me," he said.

"Okay, then," said Byte. "My house this time."

When the bell ending lunch rang, Mattie hauled up his backpack and headed off toward his first class of the afternoon. Jake and Peter went ahead too, but Byte hung behind, gathering up her books and her laptop computer. When Jake and Peter were out of earshot, she ran to catch up with Mattie.

"So," she said, "any news on the Caitlyn front?"

Mattie shook his head.

"None at all? You must have talked to her today."

"I *listened* to her today," said Mattie. "Does that count?"

"And?" asked Byte.

Mattie slung the backpack over one shoulder and held its strap with both hands. "Other than the fact that I'm the biggest wimp in the world," he said, "I can't think of a thing."

Zachary Morgan reached for the 12-gauge shotgun that lay across the gun rack in the back of his truck. He hadn't fired it in a while, not since he had last visited his brother in Tennessee and the two had gone quail hunting together. He broke the weapon and stared down the barrel. This was habit; Zach really didn't need to examine the gun to know it needed cleaning before he used it again.

He strode around to the large black toolbox resting between the wheel wells in the bed of the truck and felt around for the smaller box containing the oil, rags, and brushes he would use to clean the shotgun. Once he found them, he lowered the tailgate, and sat on it, and spread out his tools. He found himself whistling softly as he poured oil onto one of the rags.

When he heard footsteps crunch in the soil behind him, he stopped whistling. He looked over his shoulder to see Jerry leaning against the truck as if he might fall over from exhaustion.

Jerry pointed at the gun. "What are you doing?" he asked.

Zach looked at him for a moment, saying nothing, then continued oiling the gun's bore.

"Don't ignore me, Zach," said Jerry. "I asked you a question."

Zach took one of the wire-handled brushes and slid it in and out of the barrel, clearing the gun of any traces of debris. "You know what I'm doing," he said. "Those monkey-wrenchers are bound to come back. I'm going to be ready for them."

For several moments the two men said nothing. Zach, finished with the cleaning, took the first of four shells and slid it into the weapon's magazine. He pushed it in with his thumb, feeling it click into place. One by one the others followed. Though each shell weighed little, the four of them, Zach thought, gave the gun extra heft and balance. He raised it to his shoulder and peered down the barrel, focusing on a blue jay that screeched from a nearby tree. He pressed the trigger, and the gun clicked.

"It's been a while," he said absently. "Feels good." He chambered the first shell, readying the gun to fire. Then he looked again at Jerry. "What did you want to see me about?"

Jerry stared down at the dirt for a very long time. When he looked up, his expression was one Zach did not recognize. It was not anger, for Jerry's anger came plain and straightforward, as everyone who ever experienced it knew. It was not exactly sadness—though it might have been sadness tinged with something else. Regret, maybe? Resignation? Zach waited.

"If you do this," Jerry said, "if you kill these monkey-wrenchers, you'll end everything. Even if they do intend to ruin this operation—even if they were the ones who killed Tim—nobody will understand except us. The people out there…" He waved his arm, indicating the world outside their narrow community of loggers. "They won't see it as self-defense. They'll read the story in the papers, and they'll call *us* the murderers. It will be the end of Monarch. Don't you see that?"

Zach just stared at him. "I suppose you're right," he said evenly, "but we also have to live with ourselves. Maybe you can do that, knowing that monkey-wrenchers came into our camp and killed one of our men and got away with it." He replaced the shotgun in the gun rack, clamping down the lock forcefully. "But I can't. I still get nightmares." He looked across the way at one of the other loggers. Eli had begun work on a tree and looked as though he needed a little help. Zach gestured toward him. "I better get back to work," he said.

He walked away, leaving Jerry behind him. He didn't bother to look back over his shoulder.

Jerry had come to Zach with an argument against killing those monkey-wrenchers, but in his heart he agreed with Zach's thinking—at least partly. And if Jerry didn't fully agree that these monkey-wrenchers must be punished, he *did* understand. Zach was certain.

As Zach approached, Eli withdrew the saw from the partly cut tree and waited. Zach waved him aside, and the old-timer shut down the saw's motor.

Eli had joined Monarch Lumber when Jerry's father owned the business almost thirty years ago. Zach did not know how old Eli was. Eli never spoke of retiring, and neither Zach nor Jerry would mention the idea to him. He had to be at least ten years older than Jerry, who was fifty-three, but Eli never spoke of his age, never complained of aches and pains, and went out of his way to hide from the other men the assortment of prescription bottles in his duffel.

"You feel like driving into town later tonight?" Zach asked.

Eli remained silent, waiting for an explanation. "Town" meant Bugle Point, which was almost ninety minutes away.

Zach looked around to make sure the other men weren't watching too closely. The conversation would have to be short. "It has to do with what we talked about earlier," he said. "The monkey-wrenchers. To get to them we have to get to the reporter. I'll need your help." Zach knew he didn't have to say anything more. If it meant stopping monkey-wrenchers from attacking the site, Eli would do whatever was necessary.

Eli nodded. Without asking a single question, he pulled the starter cord for the chainsaw's motor, and the two men went back to work.

Forensics Lab
Bugle Point Police Department

Marco Weese gazed down into the microscope. When he raised his head, his glasses slipped off the tip of his nose, clinked against the scope's eyepiece, and dangled against his chest from the twelve-inch length of surgical tubing he used as a strap. He put them back on without a thought, then pressed them on his nose with his index finger as if by doing so he might glue them into place.

So much of what Marco did in the lab was routine—fingerprint matching mostly, some chemical analysis, occasional blood typing; he had been doing it all so long he could almost let his mind wander as he worked. Like now. As he studied the specimen of hair under the microscope *(Oddly twisted at the base, as though it had had once been knotted. Your suspect wears a toupee, Lieutenant.)*, he thought not of suspects or toupees, but of his wife, his upcoming vacation, and his beloved birds. Perhaps he could talk her into going, yet again, to San Juan Capistrano to watch the return of the swallows.

Stain the slide. Look again. Note the bleeding of color. Your suspect also dyes his hair.

This particular afternoon, however, something nagged at the back of Marco's mind like a gnat buzzing at his ear. This feeling, this sense that he had somehow overlooked something, bothered him as nothing else could. He was a scientist, a professional. Mistakes, Weese thought, were for people whose jobs were more…*subjective.*

This feeling was enough to get him running through his day's work in his mind: the typing of blood found on a knife at a crime scene *(O negative)*, the lifting of fingerprints from the window of a stolen car *(matched to a known thief)*…and of course the hair. He envisioned himself running through the tests again, checking each procedure in his mind. He had not made a mistake.

Yes, he thought as he worked, *San Juan Capistrano would be nice.* The mission itself was lovely—and the birds! Goodness, the birds! The way they arrived—a great cloud of white fluttering down from heaven and 'anding before your eyes, settling on the mission roof, in the trees, along the pathways. The endless cooing that, when multiplied by many hundreds of swallows, sounded almost like a purr. And the feathers scattered everywhere! Tufts of white lying on the ground, blowing in the breeze, captured by a bush. Thousands of feathers. Weese could see them in his mind: White. Wispy.

Feathers…

His head whipped around to face a counter that lined one wall. The motion threw his glasses off again. He ignored them, letting them dangle against his chest and snag his tie.

He could see it even from here, lying on the counter next to the autoclave and his box of Flaky Flix: the evidence bag containing the feather. The girl, Byte, said it had come from a belted kingfisher, but Weese had never confirmed that fact for himself. Besides, why should he not have believed her? She seemed well informed, well intentioned.

As he strode toward the counter, he whispered the word *dodo,* referring to himself. His work, for once, had been sloppy. Would he neglect to check the fingerprints on a gun just because a credible witness said "There's the murderer"? Never!

He grabbed the evidence bag and once again held it to the light, examining the feather. It looked just as it had before, gray flecked with bits of dried matter. Weese also noted the dotting of white at the feather's tip, and he nodded to himself.

Here, finally, was the detail that had nagged at him all afternoon: that odd bit of color. *Unusual for a belted,* he thought. The girl said she had identified the bird from a field guide, but that meant nothing. She was untrained, inexperienced in the field. She could easily miss the subtle differences between species.

He went to his desktop computer and began a Web search. He found several Web sites devoted to birds, and he quickly perused each one. Perhaps twenty minutes passed before he found a site that was as thorough as he needed. It was so thorough, Weese had to conquer his natural urge to browse the site like a giddy online shopper. *Kingfishers,* he reminded himself, *focus on the kingfishers.*

He found several species listed—each one illustrated by a photo of the bird and a description of its size, color, behaviors, and habitats. Weese studied them one at a time, his patience strained by the slowness with which the pictures downloaded.

He stopped at the fourth.

Weese stared at the vibrant photo. Because of his nearsightedness, he found himself moving closer and closer to the monitor, until his nose was barely inches away from the glass. He suddenly realized what he was doing, and his hands scrabbled for his eyeglasses.

Weese nodded. Yes. The girl *had* made a mistake—a critical one, if his theory was correct. He had no way of knowing for certain, without seeing one of the birds up close, but his suspicions were strong enough that he decided to act on them. If nothing else, he was sure the girl and her three male friends would want to see what he had discovered.

Now where did I put that card? Weese patted down the pockets of his lab coat, feeling for the business card Byte had left him. Except for a Cross pen and a loose breath mint, his pockets were empty. He searched the lab, finally finding the card tucked between the pages of the book he had been reading during his break. *Salzmann, that was it. Byte Salzmann.* He found the e-mail address Byte had scribbled on the back of the card and prepared to send her a note. He really did have a good deal of work to do, and he had spent far too much time on this kingfisher business already. So instead of explaining to Byte what he had found, he merely typed a quick message: *This may interest you...* Then he added, without further comment, a hyperlink to the Web page. It was the most help he could offer. Now Byte would only have to open her e-mail, click on the link, and she would be able to see exactly what Weese was seeing right now.

He hoped it would be enough.

Hmm...Dromoceryle alcyon, he thought. *I wonder if those kids will know that this changes everything.*

chapter nine

rebecca Kaidanov did not smile. Mac, her editor, sat in his office with his loafers kicked off. He raised his long legs one at a time and set them on the desktop, crossing his feet at the ankles. Rebecca could see his toes clenching and unclenching thoughtfully within the red, yellow, and blue argyle socks he wore.

He was reading, for the third time, the story she had written about the press conference with Victor Madison. Perhaps he was intentionally teasing her, or perhaps it was her own impatience for his response that made it seem as though he was taking a ridiculously long time to finish. As he read, Rebecca stood on the other side of the desk, *click click click*ing the button on her ballpoint pen.

Mac finally looked at her over the edge of the paper. He stared at her for a long time, then he let the paper drop to his desk. He picked up a pencil and tapped its eraser against his knee three times—a sign that he had formed his opinion.

"Not bad," he said.

Rebecca finally allowed herself the smile. Her fingers relaxed around the pen. "I knew you'd love it," she said. "So now you have to say something else, too."

Mac leaned back and placed his hands behind his head, studying her. "And what would that be?" he asked.

"You have to say, 'All right, Rebecca, you've taken this first step. The story is yours.' You have to promise you won't throw it off to a more experienced reporter if this turns into something big."

Mac smiled a little himself, though Rebecca wasn't quite sure if he was appreciating her tenacity or just quietly laughing at her zeal. "The story is yours," he said. "Though I'm not sure how much bigger a story you'll find. 'Victor Madison Collapses at Press Conference' is good, but it might be all there is."

No problem, Rebecca thought. The point was that, one way or another, she would be the one to find out.

She grinned all the way to the parking lot. *Three o'clock. Just time enough to run a few errands and get a bite to eat before finishing up the story tonight.* She continued to smile when she climbed into her Geo Tracker and threw in her favorite Billy Joel CD, a concert performance in Moscow. The smile faded only slightly when Joel strummed the opening chords of Dylan's "The Times They Are a-Changin'"—a song of protest that reminded Rebecca a little too much of her father. How proud he would be of his little girl! Rebecca cranked up the volume, singing along at the top of her lungs.

She picked up take-out on the way home.

She stopped at the dry cleaner to pick up a skirt.

She paused at the foot of the stairs to get her mail.

A few moments later, when she fumbled with her keys and pushed open her apartment door, she sensed movement on the other side. The sensation was only a flicker, not enough to stop her and turn her around. Before she could think about what it meant, someone's arm yanked her in and locked around her waist. A hand clamped down over her mouth to muffle her screams.

Two men in black ski masks grabbed Rebecca and threw her against a wall. She heard a ripping sound, like cloth tearing, and realized one of the men had pulled a strip of heavy duct tape from a thick, silvery roll. The hand left her mouth, and the strip of tape took its place. She tasted glue on the tip of her tongue.

While one man held her against the wall, his forearm pressed into her neck and the underside of her chin, the other pulled at her reporter's satchel and at the leather bag containing her laptop. Her skirt, fresh from the cleaners and still in its plastic bag, crumpled to the floor. The take-out container landed beside it, spilling sweet and sour chicken onto the carpet near her feet.

"This is so you learn to mind your own business," hissed a voice.

The man holding her satchel turned it upside down and emptied it contents. He ignored her makeup, her ID carrier, her press card, and her checkbook, reaching instead for her life's blood—the microcassette recorder, the Day-at-a-Glance, and the spiral notebook. He opened the notebook first and flipped through it, examining each page. Then he took out a disposable cigarette lighter and set the notebook on fire. As the flames reached his fingers, he dropped the book into the steel wastepaper basket next to Rebecca's desk. Her appointment book, the Day-at-a-Glance, followed. All her connections, her phone numbers and addresses, her appointments—the very life of a reporter—went up in flames. Rebecca closed her eyes. An acrid scent filled the room as the book's vinyl binding melted.

She opened her eyes a moment later to see that he had grabbed her microcassette recorder. He slipped it from its case and stomped on it with his heavy black boot. The plastic cracked. He stomped on it a second time, shattering the outer case and breaking the tiny circuit board inside. Rebecca watched as the wheels that drove the tape spilled out and rolled across the floor. The man then reached for the tiny cassette inside the machine. He pulled the tape from inside the cassette, unspooling it yard after yard. He tore it to bits in his fingers and dropped the torn lengths into the flames. Her other cassettes, even the new ones still in their shrink-wrap, followed.

No…

Rebecca watched, silent, as the man destroyed everything. He took the floppy diskettes from her desk and cracked open each one, tearing the tiny disks from within the cases. He pulled a claw hammer from a tool loop on his jeans and swung it against her laptop computer—first the screen, then the keyboard. The tiny plastic letters arced across the room like fleas escaping the back of a dog. When he was finished, he took the hammer to her desktop computer as well. He swung it against the monitor first, showering her desktop with broken glass. Then he pounded at the CPU, denting the outer steel case. As he worked, the computer collapsed in on itself, almost folding in half.

Finally, the man held up a small object. He stood near a wall and waved his arm. A loud hissing, like air escaping from a tire, accompanied this motion. Rebecca watched as huge letters in red spray paint appeared against the light wallpaper.

Then the man, his breath heaving from him, looked at the other. He nodded as if to say *It's finished.*

The man with the hammer then joined his partner, and the two of them shoved Rebecca to the floor. One wrapped her wrists with the duct tape, then her ankles. *Strange,* she wondered, *that they didn't do this sooner.* Then, as suddenly as the thought occurred to her, she understood the answer. If the men had bound her earlier, she might have found it difficult to see what they were doing. And they wanted her to see.

"Don't forget this," said one of them. "And tell your monkey-wrencher friends."

Then quietly, like guests leaving a party early, they slipped out the door and were gone. Rebecca—her wrists, ankles, and mouth still bound with tape—began to weep. The crying came from fear mostly, and in a few minutes the fear spent itself. Rebecca felt a change come over her. She reached her bound hands to her mouth, squeezed her eyes shut, and tore the duct tape away from her face. Then, spitting to rid her mouth of the taste of adhesive, she began working on the tape at her wrists. She dug at it with her teeth, tearing away a bit of it, then working the tear until she could pull her wrists apart. She then unwrapped the tape from her ankles.

Her first impulse was to pick up the mess the men had made, but she immediately saw how foolish that would be. The glass on her desktop, the broken remnants of her computers, even the spilled take-out were pieces of evidence, any one of which might serve to catch the men who had hurt her. She consoled herself with one bit of cleaning, however: she picked up her freshly cleaned skirt, smoothed out the wrinkles, and hung it in her bedroom closet.

Then she picked up the phone.

Her hair had come loose in the back, and a great mass of it had fallen across her face. Rebecca ran her hand through it, pushing it from her eyes, and punched in the number for the police.

And later, after she had spoken with the police, she would call those high school kids to find out exactly what they had gotten her into.

"So where exactly *are* we?" asked Jake. He reached into a bowl of popcorn Byte had placed on the coffee table and stuffed a handful into his mouth.

Byte had been asking herself the same question. So much had happened—gunshots in the forest, FBI agents knocking on Peter's door in the middle of the night, a congressman working behind the scenes.

And the birds. Something was killing the birds. Byte occasionally wondered if the Misfits hadn't finally run into a mystery they could not solve—that the odds against them were too great, the enemy too strong. But now, as she was most filled with doubt, she thought of the dead kingfisher. She remembered the way it lay in her hand, weightless as straw. The image of the bird would not let her go.

"Let's review," said Peter. He sat forward as he spoke, his elbows braced against his knees and his hands clasped in front of him. His hair fell across his face, and instead of sweeping it away he gazed at his friends from behind it. "We know there's a group of men in the woods, and we know they're involved in some sort of questionable activity."

"Which we figure is logging, right?" asked Mattie.

"Right," said Jake, "because they called us monkey-wrenchers."

Peter nodded. "It's the simplest theory we have that fits all the facts."

As she listened, Byte found herself shaking her head. *No,* she was thinking, *no to all of this. The congressman doesn't matter. Monkey-wrenchers don't matter. The men in the woods don't matter.*

Someone had placed a CD in her mom's minisystem, and Byte suddenly found the noise painful. She grabbed a remote from the coffee table and fired it in the direction of the shelf. The music stopped. The Misfits, caught in the silence, turned toward her.

"I don't care about any of that," Byte said flatly. "What I really want to know about is the birds. We've been chased and shot at. We've gone to a reporter. We've asked a police scientist to help us. *And we still don't know why the birds are dying!*"

The others stared at her without speaking. Byte's eyes flickered from one Misfit to the next, measuring what each might be thinking. "Okay," she said. "Why aren't you saying anything?"

Jake shrugged and offered half a smile. "I don't know what to say," he said. "I don't think I've ever seen you this mad before."

"I *am* mad," said Byte. "I mean, I'm frustrated. We're not accomplishing anything."

Peter nodded his agreement. "I have to admit I'm a little frustrated myself. I'm not exactly sure where to go next."

His fingers toyed with a popcorn kernel. Peter was hesitating in a way that was unnatural for him. Unnatural, Byte thought, because it suggested that Peter did not have confidence in his own ideas. Byte absolutely hated the uncertainty she saw in his eyes. "Come on, Peter," she said. "Snap out of it. You're our big idea person."

"Okay," said Peter, "okay." He sat up straighter and spoke with a little more energy. "I suppose we could go back online and check out the rest of Congressman Madison's Web site. We might learn something there."

"Good. That's good," said Byte.

She slipped over to her desktop computer and flicked on the power. Though she doubted the Misfits would find anything, it felt good to try.

She clicked on her Internet provider, and hours seemed to pass before the sign-on screen came up. *Click on the icon. Type in your code.* She was just getting ready to key in the address for Congressman Madison's Web site when—

You've got mail!

"Better check it out," said Byte. "Might be from my mom."

She opened the mailbox and saw a single piece of mail from someone who called himself "Birdman." Frowning, Byte clicked on the envelope icon.

"Hey, it's from Weese," she said. "It just says, 'This may interest you.'"

"That's it?" asked Jake.

"No, wait. There's a link to a Web page. Hang on."

Byte clicked on the blue address Marco Weese had placed at the bottom of the e-mail, and a moment later her screen resolved into a color photo of a kingfisher ruffling its wings to shed them of water.

Jake stood at Byte's shoulder and pointed at the screen. "Hey, that's our bird."

"Yes, it is," said Peter. He frowned and shook his head. "But we've already identified the bird. Why would Weese send us this?"

Byte heard the conversation but paid little attention. Her eyes scanned the text at the bottom of the photo. Here was the common name of the species, the formal Latin name, some discussion of the bird's habits, and a map of the U.S. bearing a tiny red dot—the place where the species might be found.

A single dot. In northern Oregon.

Byte swallowed. "Guys?" she said quietly.

"Maybe he's just confirming what we told him," Jake suggested. "Just to let us know we were right."

"Mayyyybe," said Peter, but the way he said the word suggested he wasn't convinced.

"*Guys*," said Byte. Her fingernail ticked against the screen where she pointed. "I think you better look at this."

Mattie scooted next to Byte and read from over her shoulder. "Warren's kingfisher. *Dromoceryle alcyon.*"

Peter moved closer to the screen and studied the picture. "That's definitely our bird," he said. "So it's not a belted kingfisher at all."

"I guess the two species just look a lot alike," said Byte. "But check this out…"

Below the name of the bird was a tiny red flag that blinked on and off. Next to the flag were the words "One-hundred and fifty known breeding pairs."

Byte looked at her friends, and she could tell by their

166 blank faces that none of them—not even Peter—fully understood what they were seeing. "Guys," she said, "this bird is an endangered species. Only a few of them are left, and those are somewhere in Oregon. I don't think anyone even knows they're here in Pine Bluff." She clicked on a button, and the image of the bird grew larger, filling the entire screen.

Peter nodded. "No one," he added, "except for the person who's killing them."

They looked at one another, the silence broken only when, a moment later, the phone began to ring.

chapter
ten

Peter pointed to an upstairs apartment. "There," he said.

Rebecca had given Byte scattered directions over the phone, hesitating and often repeating herself. Byte said the reporter had been crying, and that she'd hesitated several times, struggling to remember whether a particular turn was a right or a left. Now Peter broke into a run as he headed toward the wrought-iron staircase that led to the second floor. A reporter would not have trouble with such details, he knew, unless something was terribly wrong. Byte and Mattie followed him up the staircase, their feet clattering on the metal risers. Jake took up the rear and moved more slowly, his eyes scanning the parking lot and the apartment grounds.

Peter pounded on the door. "Rebecca," he called out. "It's us."

The door swung open only a few inches, caught by a brass security chain, and a pair of eyes peered out. The door then slammed shut, and the chain rattled. When it opened again, it swung wide, and Rebecca Kaidanov gestured the Misfits in.

"Watch your step," she said.

Once the Misfits were inside, Peter saw Rebecca more clearly. Her hair looked ratty, and she kept running her hand through it. Dark circles rimmed her eyes and bled in long lines down her cheeks, the remains of mascara that had dissolved from her crying. A faint bruise had formed along her neck.

Peter gazed about the room. Spatterings of white fingerprint dust lay everywhere. Shards of glass blanketed the carpet. A few feet away on the desktop, the bashed remnants of a computer lay crumpled next to the hollow shell of a monitor. Tiny bits of plastic littered the living room floor, and Peter slowly came to realize they were keys broken from two computer keyboards. Shattered casings from computer diskettes were strewn all around, as if someone had snapped them in two and thrown them in a rage.

"Oh, my God," said Byte. "Rebecca, what happened?"

The reporter's face was flat and expressionless. "I guess someone didn't like my story."

Jake bent down and reached for one of many circular pieces of vinyl that lay on the floor. He held it up to the light, showing the others that the vinyl was torn. It was the data disk from inside one of the broken floppies. Jake turned his gaze toward Byte. "Any chance of saving these?" he asked.

Byte shook her head.

"Apparently," said Peter, "we've made some people very nervous—or angry." He turned toward Rebecca. "I'm sorry."

Rebecca seemed to smile just a little. "My father was a reporter in the USSR. He had his nose broken four times by KGB. Once, when I was only three or four, one of them came to our house and put his hand on my cheek. He looked at my father and said, 'It would be a shame if anything happened to such a sweet little girl.'" She gestured, then, at the damage to her apartment. "So you see, this should be nothing to me."

"Peter," said Byte, "this is *our* fault. We have to do something."

Peter nodded. The Misfits had suffered some close calls themselves, but this was the first time someone had gotten hurt just for helping them. He studied Rebecca. Her hand trembled as she once again ran it through her hair.

"How long ago did this happen?" he asked.

She shrugged. "Twenty minutes ago. I called you right after I called the police."

"What'd they say?" asked Mattie.

Rebecca snorted. "They took a report."

Peter nodded to himself. "The answer is in Pine Bluff," he said. "That's where we'll find whoever did this. That's where we'll solve our mystery. I'm sure of it."

"If we leave now, we can make it before dark," said Byte.

Peter frowned. If they were going back into the woods, he would like to plan first. He would like to be ready, to have certain precautions in place. On the other hand, the men who did this had only a twenty-minute lead. Would they expect someone to follow them so quickly? Would they expect anyone to follow them at all? Leaving now, the Misfits would reach Pine Bluff—no doubt where the men were headed—shortly after the men themselves. The close timing could be a great advantage.

Peter looked at his friends. "All right, then. We've got to try to catch up with those men. The faster we can make up for lost time, the less chance they'll have to finish whatever it is they're doing."

"What's the plan?" asked Mattie.

"I don't know. I'm making this up as I go along." Peter looked again at Rebecca. "Really—we're sorry."

He strode toward the door, but just as his fingers closed on the knob, Rebecca's voice stopped him. "Wait!"

The Misfits turned.

"Before you go," said Rebecca. "The men—well, they left a message. I think it's for you."

She took a step backward and gestured toward a section of wall at the opposite end of the room. The Misfits had focused so much on the damage around the reporter's work area, they had not seen the single word sprayed on the far wall in glistening red paint:

Monkey-wrenchers.

Jake remained silent as Peter drove. His hands felt jittery, so to calm himself he began thinking of "Mood Indigo," a Duke Ellington number he had been working on in jazz band class. He closed his eyes and tried to recall the piece. His hands, obedient, fell into place just as though they were gripping his antique clarinet. He moved his fingers, popping them up and down, rolling them in a slow, undulating series of trills, all the while hearing the music in his mind. But after only a few moments of this exercise, his fingers seemed to lose track of what they were doing. He tried to listen, to find the music again, but he couldn't. He was just moving his fingers stupidly. He took a very deep breath, held it for only a moment, then let it escape. It fogged the window, and he swiped at the glass with a shirtsleeve.

When he glanced over his shoulder at Mattie, he noticed that the younger boy had slipped a deck of playing cards from his jacket pocket. Mattie riffled them, then he began making the top one disappear, reappear, disappear, reappear…

"I don't exactly want to be the party-pooper around here," said Mattie, "but are we all remembering that the last time we tried this, someone shot at us?" The card disappeared again.

"Actually," said Peter, "I've been thinking about that quite a bit. Let me ask you something: The last time they shot at us, did any of us get hit?"

Jake looked at him. "Do we have to actually get hit for it to be a problem?"

"No—I'm serious," said Peter. "They had a rifle. Presumably they knew how to use it. Could they have shot one of us if they had wanted to?"

Byte shook her head. "I don't get your point. It was dark. We were all wearing black…"

"Right," said Peter, "but they had high-powered flashlights and a rifle. Jake was huffing through the woods at about half a mile an hour with Mattie sprawled across his shoulders. So couldn't they have shot one of us if they had wanted to?"

No one answered.

"My point exactly," said Peter. "We're not supposed to be dead. We're supposed to be *scared*."

The truck's tires spit out dirt and gravel as Zach Morgan pulled it onto the work site. It jerked to a stop, shuddering a few seconds even after Zach had turned off the key. It was getting old, and Zach had driven it hard on this trip.

He and Eli stepped from the truck's cab and glanced at each other. The hammer was back in its toolbox, and the black ski masks lay in a gas station dumpster somewhere outside Bugle Point. The job was done. They had destroyed property and terrified a young woman— something neither man had ever wanted to do—but they had also sent an important message.

From several feet away, the door to the portable office slammed shut and footsteps banged down the three metal steps. Jerry walked toward them, looking every bit like a father whose teenage sons had brought the car home after curfew.

"I'll handle this," Zach whispered.

Jerry looked first at Zach, then at Eli. "Where've you been?" he asked.

Zach heard no anger in the tone, no condescension. Instead, the question seemed to stem from mere curiosity, or perhaps concern. Still, Zach felt his temper flare a bit. What right did Jerry have to ask him where he'd gone, or what he'd been doing?

"Into town," Zach replied. He would say nothing more.

Jerry stiffened a bit at the curt answer, and he looked for a moment as though he might push the issue until he got a response that satisfied him. Zach stared at his old friend eye-to-eye, and Jerry's posture sagged a bit.

"It'll be dark soon," Jerry said. "One more run, and then we'll call the men in."

Zach turned toward Eli. "You heard him. And post guards. We'll watch in shifts."

"I don't think that's necessary anymore," said Jerry.

"And see that everyone who has a gun brings it," added Zach. "We don't want to take any chances."

Eli nodded and walked off. Zach knew the old-timer would be thorough, especially in regards to the weapons. Zach had his shotgun and a hunting rifle ready, and after Tim had died, one or two of the men had taken to keeping handguns. Eli was one of them. Zach turned back to Jerry. "Anything else?"

Jerry's eyes flickered curiously across Zach's face. He paused before answering. "No," he said. "No, I guess not."

Peter was grateful that his mother was a bit more of a pushover than his father was. It had taken only a few minutes of his best "lawyering" to get his car keys back.

He guided his '69 Volkswagen convertible off the freeway and onto a two-lane highway that wound into the woods. He followed this highway for several miles, his tiny car fighting every inch of the sharp curves and steep uphill climb. Near the top of the climb, he found the ranger station and the entrance to the campground. Beyond that was nothing but the darkening forest.

"Do we have a plan yet?" asked Byte.

"Same as before," said Peter.

Jake let out a snort. "Can't really argue with success, I suppose."

Peter looked at Jake and smiled. "Tonight will be different. Trust me."

From the back seat, Mattie muttered, "I hate it when he says that."

The winding road came to an end. The Volkswagen crept toward the tiny parking lot connected to the ranger station. Peter, eyeing the cool glow of the fluorescent light through the windows, thought of Ranger Tummins. If Tummins were any kind of law enforcement officer at all, he would remember a vintage cherry-red Beetle.

"We'll park in the campground," said Peter.

Amid the camper trucks, the lumbering Winnebagos, and the monstrous SUVs, the Volkswagen seemed truly like a bug. Nestled between the larger vehicles, it would be all but invisible to anyone in the ranger station.

Jake was the first to get out of the car. He stood stretching his arms and arching his back, his muscles needing relief from the cramped space inside the VW. He walked toward the weatherworn steps that lay at the base of the hiking trail, and the others fell in behind him. Byte was the last. She came to a halt at the bottom step. Peter glanced over his shoulder and watched her as she placed her hand on the wooden rail and stared at the trees.

"What's different?" she asked. Her voice was quiet, as though she wasn't really talking to anyone but herself.

"Hmm?" said Peter.

"Oh…I was just looking at the woods," said Byte. "Remember how the trees looked when we were here last Sunday afternoon—so bright, with the sun coming through the branches?" She shook her head. "I don't know. They look different now—all dark, I mean. Makes me sad."

She glanced again at the trees, then followed Peter up the stairs.

Use it if you have to, Eli had said.

Joshua Kindel—Josh to everyone in the lumber camp—hefted the chromed, 9mm semiautomatic handgun and stared at the name embossed on the barrel. Beretta. He didn't know what it meant. The only Beretta he knew had a Chevy logo on it. Josh pulled back the

176 slide and was surprised at the stiffness of the spring. It took nearly all the strength in his fingers to draw the slide to the point where it stopped and a bullet snicked into the chamber. When he let the slide go, it snapped back into place like the teeth of a bear trap. He was afraid the gun would go off, the way the slide rebounded, but Eli said you were supposed to handle a semiautomatic that way.

Use it if you have to.

Josh didn't want to carry the gun in his hand—might make him look too nervous. Or he might drop it and have it go off. *That* would show Eli and Zach he knew what he was doing! They'd be laughing about that around the mess table until Josh was old enough to have arthritis. Mortified at the thought, he slipped the gun into his belt.

Guard duty. First time. Josh hated the whole idea, but it was his turn. How was he supposed to recognize a monkey-wrencher anyway? What did one look like? And what exactly was he supposed to do if he saw one?

His hand hovered, shaking, near the gun's rubber handgrips. He supposed he would just do what Eli said. He and Zach knew best. And if a monkey-wrencher did show up—then well, that would just be too bad for the monkey-wrencher.

The trail had darkened.

Peter paused and stared up through the tree branches. *Good.* The sun was lower in the sky, but it wasn't dark yet.

"Where are we?" asked Mattie.

"Just a little past the clearing," said Byte. "Remember where we parked our bikes before? It was in that grassy area we passed five minutes ago."

Yes, Peter thought. And this was about as far as they had come. It was just ahead—just beyond the bend in the trail—where the men had stepped from the woods with their flashlights and their guns.

"Time to move off the trail," he said.

Peter knew it was a toss-up: The forest would provide cover, but it also would make moving more difficult. The thickness of the trees and the fullness of the spring growth would make it harder for anyone to see the Misfits as they made their way deeper into the woods. But unlike the trail, which was clear and worn down to hard-packed soil, the forest floor would have a fine coating of dry, dead pine needles and brittle twigs, a littering of small tree branches that had broken off from the wind or under the weight of last winter's snows. With their first steps, the dry crackling beneath their feet might give them away.

Jake frowned. "What's that noise?" he asked.

"I don't hear anything," said Mattie.

Jake turned first in one direction, then in another, as though honing in on the sound. Peter watched him, and just as Jake raised his arm and pointed toward the distant buzzing, Peter heard it too. All the Misfits heard. The four turned in the direction of the sound, and the buzzing slowly grew to a louder hum and then to a repetitive *whup whup whup.* Finally it became an almost unbearable roar of wind and mechanical fury as the helicopter approached them and tore over their heads, seeming to skim the tips of the trees as it passed.

The Misfits crouched in the undergrowth. As the helicopter roared over them, Peter noted the direction it took.

"What do we do now?" shouted Mattie.

Peter stood and wiped the dirt from the knees of his pants. "What else?" he asked. "We follow it."

They didn't have to follow it far—maybe two tenths of a mile. In fact, the chopper remained so close, the sound of it hardly diminished.

"Whatever that helicopter's doing," said Peter, "it's going to grab the attention of a lot of people. This is our chance to get close."

Jake pointed to his left. "The best cover is this way."

He took the lead and guided the Misfits through the thickest part of the woods. Peter couldn't tell what was going on—he saw little more than Jake's form a few feet ahead of him—but the sound of the helicopter grew louder. *It's stationary,* Peter thought, *hovering in the air.* In another few moments, he and his friends would be directly under it.

Jake turned and waved. *Here,* he seemed to be saying, *look…*

Something brushed past Peter. It was Byte, stepping ahead of him in her eagerness. She moved to Jake's side and stood on her toes to look over his shoulder. Peter, along with Mattie, joined her a moment later.

"Oh, my god," Byte said. "Oh, my god."

The helicopter hovered over what appeared to be a clearing in the woods. Peter had to study the scene a moment, absorb it, before he realized it wasn't a natural clearing at all. Tree stumps dotted the area—flat, ugly disks with roots like tentacles that snaked across the ground a foot or two before dipping down into the hard-packed soil. For a moment Peter had the ridiculous thought that they resembled a herd of wooden octopi. Men, dozens of men, brandished chainsaws whose mechanical whining became audible over the roar of the helicopter as the Misfits approached. Several trucks sat in the clearing as well, and Peter was certain he could make out in the distance one, perhaps two, portable buildings. A sign on the door of one of the trucks was a fully signed confession: In bright, clear letters it proclaimed "Monarch Lumber Co."

The Misfits watched as two men reached for thick cables that dangled from the chopper's belly. They attached these cables to a fallen tree, and a few moments later the chopper rose, burdened by the massive weight. It turned then and very slowly headed off in the direction it came.

Byte stared at the ragged stumps, and she folded her arms around her stomach. "Oh, Peter," she said, "I feel sick."

The Misfits continued to watch only another moment or two, because in the next instant a piece of bark spit up from a tree and bounced off Peter's shoulder. Peter stared at the small tear in his shirt, pulling at it to reveal a bit of scratched, bleeding skin underneath.

What just happened?

Another piece of bark chipped off the tree and pinwheeled over Mattie's head. Peter frowned, and then his eyes widened with understanding. *Of course.* The roar of the helicopter and the grinding of the chainsaws would make it impossible to hear the crack of a small handgun.

"Run," he hissed. "They're shooting at us!"

A few of the lumberjacks spotted the gunman and shut down their saws in curiosity. More joined them, and with the helicopter gone now, the only sound Peter heard was the brittle *pak pak pak* of a distant, small-bore handgun. A moment later this sound was joined by another, more powerful sound—an air-shredding roar that echoed several times before it faded. Peter recognized it as a high-powered rifle.

Upon ordering his friends to run, Peter had clasped Byte's hand and pulled her along with him. Now, from several yards away, he could hear the rush and crackle of the undergrowth as Jake and Mattie scattered.

"Come on," he said.

He and Byte ran a bit further, then crouched low and hid behind trees. The guns went silent, but Peter took the silence to mean that the gunmen were moving into the woods.

"They're stalking us," he whispered.

Byte turned to look at him, her face a flat mask. Peter could tell only that she was not thinking about the men or the guns or the immediate danger. Instead, her expression seemed to contain fragments of the entire mystery: the dead kingfisher in her hand, the stumps of the trees, the black streaks on Rebecca Kaidanov's face.

"Peter," she said, "when we get out of this, I'm going to write letters to the newspapers, post a Web site, and e-mail every environmental organization on the planet. I don't care what I have to do, but everybody—*everybody*—is going to know what's happening out here."

A crackling sound came from behind them. Peter and Byte turned just as a man stepped calmly from between two trees. He was tall—taller, even, than Jake—and he moved with the same quiet confidence. One hand was stuffed into the pocket of his jeans, and a shotgun dangled at the crook of his elbow. Peter recognized him. This was the same man who had found the dead bird inside Peter's backpack, the same man who had come to Peter's house so late at night.

"You two," the man said, "are in a world of trouble."

Peter held up his hand, as though he might ward off whatever was coming. "We're not what you think we are."

The man nodded, indicating that he accepted Peter's statement as a possibility. "If that's true," he admitted, "then I won't kill you." He raised the shotgun and pumped a shell into the chamber. "Your problem, son, is that I think you're lying."

Mattie was lost.

He remembered taking off when the first shots clipped the tree, running until his weak ankle forced him to limp. He remembered how he had pulled up, hopping on one leg when the ankle gave out completely, and how he had fallen behind a Douglas fir to catch his breath. He sat now with his eyes closed and his chest heaving. As he rested, he winced at the sound of the gunshots—some light and distant, like firecrackers popping, others low and loud and much closer.

The sky had taken on a gray cast, and Mattie couldn't be certain how far or in which direction he had run. He looked around, and he couldn't see the gunmen, or his friends, or even the huge logging camp that, barren of trees, had looked so cratered and moonlike.

He sat listening, his back against the tree and his arms folded around his head. More shots echoed, but Mattie was unable to determine their direction. One thing he did know: *He* did not seem to be a target at all. It was as though Mattie, as far as the gunmen were concerned, had vanished. He just seemed to be able to do that—disappear—whether or not he was even trying. He also knew that Byte and Peter were together. He had seen Peter grab Byte's hand before they had run off. *Good,* Mattie thought. *They can look out for each other, and Byte knows the woods.*

Mattie rose to his knees and peered into the forest. In the distance, men called to one another, as though they had found something, and Mattie suddenly realized that he no longer heard the sound of Jake crashing through the undergrowth. *Captured?* The very idea made Mattie feel like a lizard was crawling down his back. He continued to listen, but he heard only the whooing of an owl, the thrum of insects, and the faint ticking of pine needles as they blew off the trees and landed in the dirt.

Behind these sounds, he heard a faint crackling—like someone closing his fist around a dry leaf. Mattie froze, then jerked his head around when he realized the noise had come from behind him. He heard the sound again and knew exactly what it was—footsteps crunching dry pine needles. Someone was coming. Mattie slipped silently around a tree and pressed himself against the trunk. Behind him, the crunching grew louder. Mattie heard a metallic ratcheting, the slide drawing back on a handgun.

"Come out," said a voice. "Come on out. I know you're back there."

Mattie glanced first in one direction, then another. *Run, or hide?* he wondered, but in the second it took for him to arrive at an answer, it was too late. An arm swept out from behind the tree and grabbed Mattie by the shirtfront, yanking him around. Mattie found himself staring into the face of a heavyset man with a ruddy face and a thick, bull-like neck. The man pressed his arm against Mattie's chest, pinning Mattie to the tree. Mattie stopped struggling when the man held up the gun.

"Don't make me use this," the man said.

A second man stepped from the shadows and drew his face close to Mattie's. It was an old man's face—leathery like an ancient baseball mitt, and lined with a wispy, pure-white beard.

"What are we gonna do with him, Eli?" asked the gunman.

The old man stared at Mattie, shaking his head. "Just a kid," he muttered. "Take him to the camp. And tell Zach."

The rear door to the panel truck squealed open on rusty hinges. Strong hands gripped the back of Peter's shirt and shoved him inside. The hands belonged to the tall man—the man whose name, Peter had learned, was Zach. Peter landed on an oil spot on the floor of the truck bed and slid into one of the panel walls.

"The girl too," Zach said.

Byte landed next to Peter, her breath leaving her in a loud *oomph* when she fell. Peter heard the screeching sound a second time, and he drew Byte to him just as the doors slammed shut. In complete blackness, he heard the latch clamping down to seal the two of them inside.

"Are you all right?" he asked.

"Compared to what?"

Peter didn't answer. "Okay. Maybe we should crawl around here a little. This must be the truck they use to transport the hand equipment, like the chainsaws. With any luck, we might find something that'll help us get out of here."

He crawled away, and he could hear Byte fumbling around a few feet away from him. The truck was mostly chapter ten

empty, Peter decided, filled only with the few items the loggers weren't using. His hand brushed against a chain broken off one of the saws, then the saw itself. His knee bumped against a metal toolbox. He felt containers, lots of containers—and now that the door had been shut for a few moments, he smelled gasoline.

"Wait," said Byte. "This might help."

Peter heard a click, and a pale yellow light bathed the inside of the truck bed. It reflected off the steel walls, casting a mustard glow over the boxes, the metal containers, and the tools. He turned and looked at Byte. A large, boxy flashlight dangled by its handle from her index finger. The light swung back and forth a bit, and the shadows in the truck stretched and contracted, stretched and contracted.

In the eerie light, Peter thought he saw Byte smiling. "You have until the batteries go dead to get us out of here," she challenged.

He studied the double doors. Steel rods ran along the edge of each, from the floor of the truck to the ceiling. They appeared to be part of the mechanism that kept the doors locked; Peter could see where one rod dipped into a tiny hole in the floor. *That's it.* He ran his hands along the length of the rod, feeling for some kind of knob or latch. "Sometimes," he said, "these trucks have an emergency release on the inside, just in case someone gets locked in accidentally." Halfway along the edge of one door, he found a four-inch lever, about the thickness of his thumb. He pressed his palm against it and pushed

186 upward. The rod moved a fraction of an inch, lifting from the hole then slamming back down. Peter tried a second time.

"*Ooof.* It won't move any higher. They must have put a lock through the handle outside."

"Can we use anything in here?" She swept the light along the floor of the truck.

Peter took a quick inventory. The broken chainsaw was useless—as was the toolbox, he was afraid. He had seen no removable screws in the truck's steel doors, nothing to take apart. *A hacksaw,* he told himself, *could cut through the steel rod...* "Let me see the light for a minute," he whispered to Byte. He flipped open the toolbox and found only some screwdrivers, pliers, wire cutters, Allen wrenches, a single pair of channel-locks, and several odd-looking tools he did not recognize—probably used in the maintenance of the chainsaws.

"Not much help here," he said. He sat next to Byte, his back against one of the panel walls.

"Any other ideas?" she asked quietly.

Peter shook his head. The gesture was more than just a "no" to Byte's question. It was frustration leveled at everything—at the logging, at not knowing where Jake and Mattie were, at the dying kingfishers, at being stuck in a hot, stuffy truck bed that stank of oil and gasoline.

"I'm afraid Mattie's better at this sort of thing," was all he said.

In the reek of gasoline, he could hardly think. The smell came from several large, metal cans that lined the opposite wall of the truck. *Fuel for the chainsaws,* Peter told himself. The cans looked ancient, their red finish scratched and soiled with grime. Next to the last can lay a burlap sack, draped over what appeared to be several smaller containers.

Peter frowned. "What's that?"

"Hmm?"

He pointed at the sack. "See that? What do you suppose that is?"

Byte looked at him, silent. She crinkled her nose to keep her wire-framed granny glasses from slipping, then finally threw up her hands. "Fine," she muttered, "I'll look. Typical guy. When a girl's around, you expect her to do everything."

Before Peter could defend himself and the rest of the male species, Byte scooted across the truck bed and snatched the sack away. Beneath it was a yellow plastic container, the shape of a gallon milk jug, only larger. Shredded white paper clung to one side of the container where someone had torn off the label. Byte unscrewed the lid, and a sickly sweet smell—tainted with the scent of something odd and dangerous—wafted through the tiny space.

"Pshew!" Byte said, screwing the lid down quickly, "smells like the stuff my grandfather used to spray in his garden to keep the bugs off the tomatoes."

"Pesticide?" Peter brushed away the hair that had fallen in a clump across his forehead as his mind raced. *Pesticide. Why would a logging crew need pesticide?*

188   Then, an instant later, he knew. It was as though a book had landed *splat* in front of him, its pages open.

"I've got it," he said.

"Hmm?"

"I've got it, Byte. I know what's happening to the birds."

chapter eleven

Spiked with adrenaline, Jake ran. His large frame—large *target*, he reminded himself—crashed through the brush. The tinier branches raked his skin, leaving a web-like pattern of scratches along his face and neck.

Run, he told himself, *and keep running. Find the trail. Find the others. Get to the car.* The air tore with rifle fire, and the ground in front of Jake fountained upward. He lurched to the left and kept running. The wind seemed to howl; twigs snapped. Jake stepped on a dead branch, and it cracked like a pistol shot. Or perhaps it *was* a pistol shot. From a couple of hundred yards away, the rifle fired again, and this time the bullet ricocheted off a branch just above his head. His foot caught something—a root, a stone, or maybe just a clump of dry dirt. Whatever it was sent him sprawling. Jake slammed into the ground, and his head struck the base of a tree. A thick root caught him across the bridge of his nose, and when it did, a flash of sparks blasted into his field of vision, stayed a moment, then slowly dissipated.

Jake drew himself to his knees and touched his nose lightly with the fingers of one hand. Pain exploded through his sinuses. Jake grimaced and breathed deeply though his mouth. He heard a light pitter-patter, like the first few scattered drops of rain before a storm breaks, and looked down to discover that the pitter-patter was blood dripping onto the ground. He drew his hand across his nose to catch the blood, then wiped it in the moist grass.

Jake stayed on his knees, his palms flat in the dirt for support. Breathing came easier doubled over this way. And with each breath, Jake felt more able to think. What would the others do? Separated, what would they expect of each other? The obvious answer was that each member of the group would try to find the others before heading back to the car. But where were the others? And which way was the trail? In his running, had he moved closer to it, or farther away?

He heard a sound behind him and turned just as a young man approached. The young man's eyes widened upon seeing Jake. He seemed far more upset at finding Jake than Jake was at being found. The man stared at Jake, silent, and then slowly raised a gun.

"Don't move," he said, "or I'll shoot."

The gun hand trembled. The guy couldn't have been more than nineteen or twenty, Jake decided. He could have been Jake's older brother, but for the fact that he was as skinny as Peter and probably an inch shorter. Jake, still kneeling, looked over his shoulder at the man. He could see the man's fingers tightening and loosening around the gun, as though searching for a comfortable way to hold it.

"I don't want to hurt you," the man said.

Well now, that was comforting. Jake lowered his head again and saw a broken section of tree branch on the ground in front of him. It was a couple of inches in diameter and maybe eighteen inches long. Jake let his fingers wrap around it, raising it just enough to feel its weight. *Good*, he decided. *Light enough to swing quickly, but heavy enough to hurt.*

"You better get up," the man said. "I'm taking you to Zach."

Jake nodded and rose slowly. As he did, he pivoted and swung the branch around, whipping it in a tight arc that blasted the man's fingers. The man cried out, and the gun skittered across the forest floor. Jake was already moving, diving to scoop up the weapon. He grabbed it and fell on his back in the dirt, pointing the gun at the man's chest. The entire move had not taken much more than a second. The young man hadn't even moved. He just stood there, holding his injured hand, looking almost like a child who had just gotten his fingers smacked.

"Change in plans," Jake said. He tried to sound confident, but the gun felt heavy and awkward in his hand. Jake had never held one before. He thought about cocking the hammer, just for effect, but decided at the last moment that that was the *stupidest* idea he'd ever had.

The other man swallowed. He looked even younger now—and lost, like Mattie at the beginning of ninth grade. "My hand hurts," he said, as though he could think of nothing else. "I think you broke it."

Jake got to his feet and brushed the dirt from his clothing, careful to keep the gun pointed at the young man. He didn't want to hurt the guy, but he couldn't allow him to alert the others. Jake remembered the others, and the practiced way they had held *their* guns.

"What's your name?" Jake asked.

The young man looked at Jake doubtfully. After a long pause, he said, "Josh. Josh Kindel."

"Well, sorry, Josh," said Jake.

"Sorry? You mean for hurting my hand?"

Jake shook his head. "No," he said. "For this."

And he punched him in the jaw. The young man went down and did not get up.

Jake stared at the gun in his hand. He saw the way his hand shook, just as Josh Kindel's had. He tried to control the shaking but couldn't. His palm was sweaty, and the gun slid around in it like a living thing.

Jake pushed a button on the side of the gun, and the ammunition clip fell out and dropped into his palm. *How had I known to do that? Seen it on television a million times, I suppose.* He threw the clip into the woods. The gun he tossed—far—in the opposite direction.

Then he crept off to look for his friends.

Jake heard the rustling and the crackling of branches from over twenty yards away. At first he was grateful for these sounds, for the way they carried so clearly over the other noises of the forest. Only after several moments of thought did it occur to him that he should be afraid of what all the noise might mean: The loggers were no longer hiding their presence.

He moved closer to the men, tracking them by ear, moving as they moved and waiting with them when they paused. If a twig crackled beneath his foot, the sound would be lost among all the other noise. The loggers would never know he was following them.

Over the movement through the brush, he heard a voice mutter, "Hey, watch it!" and he knew it was Mattie. Jake found a hiding place and waited for the group to pass. Many of the trees stood close to a hundred feet tall, but between each were tiny saplings. Jake stayed low behind a group of these young trees and peered through their thin webbing of pine needles. He saw two men— one young, red-faced, and paunchy, the other an older man with a wispy beard trailing along his chin.

Between the two men walked Mattie.

The heavier man flattened his palm against Mattie's back and gave Mattie a terrific shove. The teen stumbled several feet, just catching himself from falling. From the look on Mattie's face, and from his silence, Jake guessed it wasn't the first time the man had pushed him.

The three walked until they once again came to the bald spot in the forest. Jake, still hiding, gazed at the littering of stumps, some the size of large tables. He saw the trucks, the neatly piled equipment, the hint of lights in the portable buildings. As he watched, the two men led Mattie to a panel truck. They opened the truck's rear doors and pushed Mattie inside. The bearded man—"Eli," the other had called him—took one last sweeping look over the forest.

"Tell Zach we've found a third." His eyes hesitated when they looked in Jake's general direction, then moved on. "I think that's the last of them." As he said this, he took a six-inch steel pin that dangled from the door of the panel truck and slipped it through a hole in the latch. "We'll decide what to do with them after dinner."

With that, the two men wandered off, and Jake could just now make out the distant hum of laughter and conversation, the almost musical clinking of glass and flatware. He waited several minutes, while the sky turned its last shades of gray before nightfall, to be certain the loggers were relaxed and full with their evening meal. Full stomachs, Jake figured, would make them slow and lazy, and perhaps less inclined to pay attention to little noises they heard. When he was certain the men were occupied, he crept from the trees and into the open area where the truck was parked. Even in the twilight it was easy to slip the pin from the latch and pop the latch up. He then gripped the handle to the door and yanked.

The hinges squealed. Jake peered into the panel truck and saw his friends' faces lit in the pale glow of a high-powered flashlight running on a dying battery. Peter, Byte, and Mattie sat huddled in the rear of the truck. Mattie's sneaker began an impatient toe-tap against the metal floor.

Jake shook his head. "And me without my camera."

Peter, ignoring the comment, stuck his nose past the door and looked around. "Where are they?"

"Eating," said Jake. "If they didn't hear me open this door."

"Let's get out of here," said Byte. "We need to get back to Rebecca and tell her what we've found."

Jake reached for Byte's hand and steadied her as she leaped from the back of the truck. Peter and Mattie followed. *The noise coming from the meal area hasn't let up,* Jake thought. *With the help of one of those flashlights, we might make it out of the woods and back home before the loggers know we're gone.*

But even as he had these thoughts, Jake once more heard the familiar ratcheting—*chu-chak!*—that comes from the pump handle of a shotgun. As if in response to the sound, he felt Mattie's hand clamp down on his shoulder. Jake turned and found himself staring at Josh Kindel. Kindel's clothes were rumpled and covered with pine needles; his hair was mussed, and a large, blue-black bruise spread across his cheek. The young man glared at Jake, and his hands gripped the shotgun with a new confidence. He pointed the barrel toward the huddled Misfits. "I'm not afraid to use this," he said.

"What are you going to do, Josh?" Jake asked. "Shoot us? What have we done?"

The young man hesitated, his hands searching for better purchase on the weapon. His fingers tightened on, then released, the shiny wooden pump handle.

"Zach!" he shouted. "Eli! Jerry! Everybody—come quick!"

In moments the loggers—over a dozen of them—surrounded the Misfits. They murmured among themselves, a low hum of conversation that Peter could not follow. The only word he could distinguish was "monkeywrenchers," a term he made out some six or seven times.

The *tone* of the men's comments was another matter. Peter sensed a wide range of attitudes among the loggers. Some—oddly enough, it seemed to be the older men—glared at the Misfits with pure hatred. Others appeared doubtful; these men gazed at their fellow workers, then at the Misfits, as though measuring Peter and his friends against what the older men had told them. A few, Peter noticed, cast a quick glance at the Misfits then stared at the ground. These were the most uncertain, the ones most frightened of the guns, the ones who would be easiest to turn to the Misfits' side if the opportunity arose. Peter noted their faces.

The logger named Zach stepped forward. "Where've you been, Josh?" he asked.

The young man looked down and hesitated before answering. "I—I've been in the woods. I've been looking for the gun Eli gave me." He pointed at Jake. "He took it from me." His fingers reached into his jacket pocket and fished out a small metal object. Peter recognized it as an ammunition clip. "Found this in the bushes. He must have thrown the gun away too."

With this, the murmuring of the men increased. It seemed they didn't quite know what to make of the fact that Jake had chosen to discard the gun rather than use it on them.

"We're not monkey-wrenchers," Peter called out. He had seen the momentary doubt on the men's faces. Now he sought to take advantage of it.

The men went silent when Peter spoke. A handful had brought guns, and these few held their weapons up as they pulled back on the slides to chamber a bullet. It was as though Zach, clearly their leader, had spoken a command to them and they had all responded.

"If we're monkey-wrenchers," Peter went on, "where are our tools?" He held his hands out to show they were empty. "Where are the knives we're going to use to cut your fuel lines? Where's the sugar we're going to dump in your gas tanks?"

The loggers were silent. A few looked at one another, clearly troubled by Peter's questions. The remainder gazed steadily at the tall man, Zach, who stood at their center. Zach scowled at Peter. "Shut up!" he barked. "You threw away the gun. You've had plenty of time to get rid of other things."

Another man stepped forward now. With his thick, wrinkled hands and white beard, he must have been the eldest member of the logging team. He gazed over the group of loggers then whispered in Zach's ear.

Zach nodded. He then pointed an accusing finger at Peter. "Don't you go playing games," he said. Peter took a small step backward. Zach's face was flushed, and his entire body quivered as though he were barely able to hold himself back from strangling the Misfits. As he pointed, his finger shook uncontrollably. "You've been out here three times now, sneaking around like thieves. You picked up one of those dead birds. You came after us at night. You broke into our camp." The list of accusations went on, concluding with Jake's "assault" on Josh Kindel.

"While we're ringing up charges," Peter said, "how about kidnapping…assault with a deadly weapon… attempted murder—"

"*Murder?*" Zach Morgan's hands curled into fists. He took a step toward Peter, then—as if by some tremendous force of will—stopped himself. The fists moved to his sides, where they remained, trembling. "You call *us* murderers? This is *our* job! *Our* place! We have the right to protect ourselves."

The men watched in silence. Some, after hearing Zach speak, glared at the Misfits and moved to the outer edges of the half-circle the group had formed. Peter suddenly understood what they were doing: He had overplayed his hand. The men would stand with their leader. If they were not entirely convinced that Peter and his friends were monkey-wrenchers, they did not have to be. It was enough that Zach believed it.

"What do you want to do now, Zach?" asked Eli. "I figure we ought to call Tummins, have these punks arrested for trespassing."

"Tie 'em up first," one of the men shouted. "Let 'em spend the night tied to a tree before turning 'em in."

"A night? Make it a week!" shouted another.

A few of the men laughed. Something small and hard flew from the middle of the crowd of men and shot toward Peter's head. He ducked, and a dirt clod exploded into dust against one of the truck panels. Another one flew a moment later and burst against Jake's shoulder. *How long*, Peter wondered, *before these men lose all sense and begin reaching for stones?* He glanced from one side of the crowd to the other, looking for an escape. The mob had pinned the Misfits against the truck. They couldn't run, and in the darkness they'd never find the path.

"Enough!"

The voice had come from the rear of the crowd of loggers. It was solid and commanding, a military officer's voice. In response, a logger's fist, caught in the spill from a flashlight, opened to let a clod of dirt fall to the ground. "Enough," said the voice again, and Peter sensed a hint of weariness. "I've heard enough." A man stepped from the back of the crowd and strode toward the front, toward the place where Zach Morgan was standing. This man was shorter than Morgan, but had a thick neck and powerful upper body. He placed his hand on Zach's shoulder, and with that touch the trembling in Zach's body visibly diminished. The man then turned toward Josh Kindel. "Put that gun down, son," he said. "You might hurt somebody." Then to the other loggers: "All of you. If you're carrying a gun, I want you to lay it on the ground. Now." Except for Eli, the men did as they were told. The man gazed steadily at Eli, and he, too, finally laid down his weapon.

The man then turned his attention to the Misfits. "I'm Jerry Vitale," he said. He gestured at the two portable buildings, the equipment, and the trucks. "This is my operation. Now why don't you tell me why you're trespassing on my work site."

It was Byte who answered. "We…we were curious. We wanted to know what was happening out here. You were trying so hard to keep it secret."

Jerry Vitale nodded. "It's more…*peaceful* that way," he said. Peter understood what he meant. Keeping the logging secret would slow down environmentalists and other protestors, people who would interfere with the work of cutting down trees. "I want you to see something," Jerry said. He pointed at a flatbed truck. The bed lay covered with what looked like small potted plants. "See that? Those are saplings. For every tree we cut down, we plant two. You can pass that along to whoever sent you. Everything I do here, I do legally. Understand?"

Peter felt his face flush. "Does that include breaking into a reporter's home?" he blurted. "Attacking her? Destroying her equipment?"

Anger passed across Jerry Vitale's face—a hint of darkness that lasted for only a moment, like the shadow of a low-flying plane. He stared at Peter. "I don't know what you're talking about."

"Someone here does," said Peter.

Jerry's eyes flickered over to Zach Morgan. The taller man eyed Peter without saying a word and did not bother to return Vitale's gaze.

"And then there's the matter of the birds," Peter added quietly.

With that, Zach's hands once again curled into fists, his fingers squeezing together as though he were trying to crush something in them.

"What birds?" asked Jerry. The man's face had lost the indignation, the sadness Peter had seen only a moment ago. Replacing it now was genuine confusion.

"You really don't know, do you?" Peter said. His eyes fell on Zach Morgan. "But *he* does."

"What birds?" Jerry asked. Then louder, to Zach: "*What birds?*" he demanded, but still Zach Morgan refused to answer. He took a step in Peter's direction, only to find himself blocked when Jerry Vitale's forearm landed against his chest. "Zach?"

"The kingfishers," Peter continued. "You know the ones." He looked at Zach Morgan. The logger's shoulders were slightly hunched, making him look weak and over-burdened. "One of your men has been pouring pesticide into the stream. It's poisoning the fish, and the sick fish are killing the birds."

"Pesticide? Why would we—?"

Byte, unable to contain herself, spoke up before Jerry Vitale could finish. "Because these kingfishers are *endangered*. If the government found out they were here, you wouldn't be allowed to cut down any more trees."

"Endangered?" Jerry whispered.

"Exactly," Peter said. He looked first at the group of loggers, then at the forest around him, then at Jerry

Vitale. "Under the Endangered Species Act, you would not be allowed to cut lumber here. The forest would have to be left as it is, to protect the birds." He slowly let his gaze fall on Zach Morgan. "So someone's been trying to kill the birds off before anyone learns they're here."

Zach took a few steps backward and in a quick motion scooped up one of the handguns left on the ground. "Shut up!" he cried. He aimed the gun at the Misfits, his thumb struggling clumsily to cock the hammer. "Do you hear me?" The gun shook in his hand. Indeed, Zach's entire body shook. His eyes were wide, the whites a sickly yellow-gold in the light from the lamps. He appeared to be trying to speak; his mouth started to form words—words of apology, words of anger—who could tell? Nothing came out. In the pale light, Peter could see Zach's finger tighten around the trigger.

Jerry Vitale reached out and placed his hand over the gun. He tugged at it gently, the way a parent might lift a toy away from a child who had fallen asleep. His palm went over the top, his fingers encircled the barrel, and he very slowly pointed the gun skyward until it lifted from Zach Morgan's hand. Zach did not speak; he did not look at Jerry. He only stared at the Misfits, his arm suspended as though he were unaware that he was no longer holding the gun.

A moment later the arm dropped limply to his side.

Ranger Tummins made the arrests.

Jerry Vitale himself made the call to the station, and in minutes Peter could make out a distant siren whining its way nearer, crawling up the steep logging road. A long period of silence followed, then a loud crackling as Tummins and another ranger stepped through the brush and into the logging camp. Zach Morgan sat at the base of a Scotch pine, his head down and his back resting against the thick trunk. Over him stood Jerry Vitale, silent, one hand still gripping the barrel of the gun he had only minutes ago lifted from Zach's fingers. Peter noticed how Vitale loomed over Morgan like a father over a disobedient child, and how Zach had seemed to shrink in his presence.

Byte whispered in Peter's ear. "I almost feel sorry for him."

Tummins spoke to Jerry Vitale for a few minutes, then strode over to where the Misfits were standing. "You four all right?" he asked. Here in the woods, Tummins seemed a little taller, a little straighter, a little more commanding than he had in the ranger station just a few nights before. The uniform even seemed to fit him better, Peter thought—or perhaps now Tummins was a better fit for the uniform.

"You knew what was going on out here," Peter said. He had meant to sound accusatory, and the tone came across.

Tummins nodded. "I knew about the logging," he said, "but not about the kingfishers or the attack on your reporter friend." He paused and rubbed his hand along his cheek while he searched for the right words. "Listen," he said, "I'm sorry about the other night. I just wanted to keep you kids out of trouble. You have to understand, the law gave Monarch Lumber the right to cut down trees out here, and my job is to enforce the law."

"What you're saying," Byte said, "is that you didn't want us nosing around because you thought you'd end up with a crowd of protestors out here."

Tummins agreed. "Basically, that's about right. I didn't want anyone to get hurt."

"But they *shot* at us!" cried Mattie.

"You were trespassing," the ranger snapped back. "And besides—" Here his head swiveled around, and his eyes searched out Jerry Vitale. The owner of Monarch Lumber was walking alongside Zach Morgan, his hand on Zach's shoulder as a ranger led the lumberman away. "You don't know the history of this company. They've earned the right to protect themselves."

The elderly logger, Eli, approached. His head tilted downward for a moment, then lifted again to stare Ranger Tummins in the eye. "Are you going to prosecute Zach for what he did?" he asked.

Tummins folded his arms and shifted his weight so that it balanced evenly on both legs. The pose was firmer than the more casual stance he had taken while chatting with the Misfits. "I figure so," he said.

"Then I guess," said Eli, "that you better arrest me too."

Tummins nodded. "Okay. Fair enough." He called to one of the other rangers. "Frank, would you cuff this gentleman, please?" Then, shaking his head in disbelief, he looked at the Misfits. "Come on," he said, "I'll give you a lift back to your car."

As they trudged through the forest toward the logging road and the ranger's squad car, Tummins glanced over his shoulder at the Misfits. He smiled at them, but the smile seemed to Peter to be a little tired and forced. "At least," the ranger said, "I won't be bothered any more by angry phone calls from congressmen's offices."

Peter's mind had been wandering, but now it snapped into focus. Ranger Tummins's words settled around him, and he found himself remembering, in perfect detail, the day of Congressman Madison's collapse. He recalled the shock, the unsteadiness and confusion on the congressman's face when Rebecca Kaidanov began her questioning. He also remembered the face of the blond man who had led Madison away, that moment when their eyes made contact.

Mattie suddenly appeared at Peter's side. "Hey, Peter," he said, "I have a question. I've been wondering about the congressman guy."

"Yeah? Me too."

"Well, I was wondering," said Mattie. "Do you think he knows about the killing of the birds and everything? I mean, shouldn't he be in some trouble too?"

Peter placed his hands on Mattie's shoulders and steered him ahead. It was too soon to know the answer, of course. They wouldn't know the whole truth until Rebecca's story about the kingfishers hit the wire services sometime tomorrow afternoon.

Yes, it was too soon to know. But Peter had a pretty strong suspicion that the kingfisher's tale was far from over.

chapter twelve

Office of Congressman Victor Madison
Congressional Office Building, Washington, D.C.
One Week Later

the whispering had been going on for days. William Benedict heard it around the office, the steady hissing behind his back when he entered each morning. He had noticed, too, the stares on the faces of the other staff members—stares that fell on him like a weight and then drifted off, as though the person had been searching for something inside William and had failed to find it. Or perhaps they had found it, and having found it had to then force themselves to look away.

The paper. A local paper. If William were saying the words aloud, he would spit them out like a mouthful of rancid milk.

The story about the kingfishers—*Warren's kingfisher, an endangered species, can you imagine?*—had appeared in the *Bugle Point Courier* six days ago. Because Congressman Madison received mention in the piece, several other papers picked up the story over the AP wire service. And because Madison was in the middle of a tight reelection campaign and had collapsed at a tele-vised press conference, the major broadcast media had also picked up the story. William had been fielding calls from CNN, Fox News, ABC, NBC, CBS, and a host of smaller broadcast outlets.

In his office, when everyone else went to lunch, William sat at his desk and ate Ruffles from a brown paper bag. With his free hand he pecked at his laptop computer, updating his résumé. The storm was coming. He had been in politics long enough to know. William sensed he had just enough time to resign from his post with the congressman and search for a position with a Washington legal firm. With his connections, he would have no problem getting the job he wanted, and once he'd left politics, he would essentially be off the hook. In Washington, resigning from politics was considered the ultimate punishment. After leaving Congressman Madison's staff, he would not be important enough to bother with.

Of course his own ambitions to be a congressman, at least for a time, would have to wait. All his efforts, all his planning, would not go to waste, but his timetable was now in ruins. He had been thinking along the lines of two years. Now he was looking at eight, perhaps ten. All because of a rookie reporter and four nosy teenagers.

William tapped out a line of his résumé, misspelled the word "coordinator," highlighted the error, then pro-ceeded to misspell the word again. He hissed between his teeth and banged out the word again.

He had not yet told the congressman that he was leaving, but he needed to soon. The timing here was crucial. If he waited too long, and someone launched an investigation of the logging in Pine Bluff, he would look like a criminal running from the bank he just robbed.

He reached for a Styrofoam cup on his desk. The chocolate cappuccino was ice-cold and sickly sweet, like a melted candy bar. He sipped it anyway for the caffeine—he hadn't slept well the last few nights—and typed some more on his résumé.

The door to the office opened, and the cup slipped in William's hand, splashing his white shirt and tie with flavored coffee. He looked up just as an elderly man with a great shock of white hair entered the room. Congressman Madison nodded a greeting to William.

"Congressman!" said William. He quickly saved his work and shut down his laptop. Only then did he begin dabbing at the coffee stain with a paper napkin. "I thought you were tied up in meetings most of the day—"

"I was, William," said the congressman. "I was."

He sat down in the chair opposite William's, lowering himself carefully and frowning once he had settled in. "Listen, William," he said. "I've made an important decision today, and I wanted you to hear it directly from me—before the rest of the staff finds out, before it appears on the six o'clock news."

"I appreciate the trust you have in me, sir."

With that the congressman went momentarily silent. He gazed at William for a very long time before continuing.

"I want you to know that I've decided to resign my seat in Congress."

"Sir?"

"My wife and I have been discussing it for some time. We both agree that it would be wrong to wait. Better to announce it now, while the election is still months away and the party can launch another candidate. I'm getting too old for this, William. I want to go home, be with my wife, visit my children and grandchildren."

"I understand, sir," said William. He had spoken with a reverence suited to the importance of the moment, but inside, William's mind was racing. Had he planned his own resignation too soon? With the congressman leaving office now, in the spring, the party would have to field a candidate quickly for the election in November. They would need someone who already had the beginnings of an organization, someone who could raise money in an eyeblink. Who could they get? Who but William had the necessary trust and familiarity with major contributors? Who but William had established such a get-it-done reputation? Assuming the nonsense about the logging went away when Madison retired, it might work. William saw his dreams coming true not in years, but in months.

"I've been thinking about you quite a bit recently, William," said the congressman. "I've been looking over the legislation you've helped me draft over the last several years, and I've taken the liberty of bringing by some gentlemen who are very eager to meet you."

Contributors? William rose from his chair, his hand absently brushing at the wet spot on his shirt. He quickly threw on his suit coat to hide the stain. "I'm ready," he said.

Congressman Madison opened the office door, and two men entered. Both wore navy blue suits that only barely hid their powerful builds. William reached out to shake their hands. The men looked at each other, shrugged, then returned the handshake.

"I'm flattered you've come," said William. "I assume you want to talk about starting a campaign fund."

One of the men reached into the inside breast pocket of his coat, withdrawing a thin, black leather wallet. "Actually…," he began. He flipped open the wallet to reveal a Justice Department ID. "We're with the FBI, Mr. Benedict. We'd like to talk to you about kingfishers."

epilogue

Bugle Point High School Cafeteria

Mattie squeezed into his wall niche and paid little attention to the lunchtime crowd. He wasn't eating. The Coke he'd so desperately wanted sat on the table next to him, the ice melting and turning the drink a light amber.

He reached into his pocket, took out a quarter, and placed it on the back of his hand, just above the knuckle of his index finger. Deftly, and without really thinking about it, he began rolling the quarter across his fingers. It moved in a series of flips from his index to his pinky, stopped, and rolled back. Mattie watched the way the coin glinted with each turn, and lost himself in the motion.

"Hey," said a voice.

He glanced up, and the coin slipped from his fingers and clattered against the Formica tabletop. Byte looked down at him, smiling. She slipped onto the bench next to him, set down her laptop computer, and tugged at the

Velcro closure on her lunch bag. It was one of those quilted fabric affairs, with a picture on the front of a rainbow-colored apple, a bite taken out of one corner. It was the logo for Apple Computers.

On a lunch bag? Mattie stared.

Byte looked down at it. "What?" she asked. "It was a promotional gift my mom got at work." Then, feigning offense: "Hey, I am not going to make excuses for my lunch bag, Mattie. You'll just have to get over it." She took out one of her veggie burgers and bit into it, apparently not minding that it was cold. Mattie shuddered.

Peter and Jake strolled up and joined them. Jake unwrapped a bacon double cheeseburger, the wax paper spotted with grease stains, and made a show out of holding the sandwich in front of Byte's face as he took the first chomp.

"Okay, carnivore," she said, smiling. "You've made your point." She pushed the burger away. "Back to your cage."

Peter sat down and sipped at his drink. "Technically," he said, "a carnivore wouldn't be eating lettuce, pickles, and tomato." Byte glared at him, and he shrugged. "Just thought you should know."

Mattie was quiet. He flipped the quarter into the air and caught it in his left fist. A moment later he opened his right hand to reveal the quarter was now *there*, then he stuffed the coin back into his pocket. He did the trick without showmanship, just a cold focus, and his friends' voices faded into background noise.

"Mattie?" A hand swatted Mattie's shoulder. "Hey—Mattie!" Mattie turned and found Jake staring at him. "What's with you? You're not talking. You're not taking apart some gizmo with your Manly-Man—"

"*Leather*man," Mattie corrected.

"Whatever. You haven't even tried to swipe one of my curly fries."

Byte grinned. "I bet I know what's bothering him." Mattie let out a short, embarrassed laugh and stared down at the tabletop as Byte ticked off the description on her fingers. "She's in the ninth grade. Cute little strawberry blond curls. Freshman Class Council officer—"

"I hear she's getting A's in *French*," Jake added. Mattie punched him in the shoulder.

"Come on, Mattie," said Peter. "Why don't you ask her out or something? It sounds like she already likes you." He tapped his finger against his chin, one of his thinking gestures. "On second thought, you could be setting yourself up for a major humiliation. Maybe you should just forget it." To punctuate the thought, he stuffed a chip in his mouth and crunched down on it.

Byte took Mattie's face in her hands. "Listen," she whispered. "If you have a chess question, ask Peter. If it's about girls, forget it, okay?"

"*Hey*," said Peter.

"All you have to do," said Byte, "is talk to her, and be yourself."

With her hands still on his face, she turned his head around so that he was looking away from his friends and down the long line of tables. Three tables down sat Caitlyn Shaughnessy. She was chattering with her friend Latisha in between bursts of writing in her Day Runner.

"You're a great guy," said Byte. "You're smart. You're cute." Mattie stood, and he felt her hands give him a gentle push.

The noise in the cafeteria—the clattering of the plastic trays, the voices, the laughter—washed over Mattie as he took those first few steps. Byte's words jabbed at him, because, truth be told, he hadn't always seen himself as smart, or cute, or any one of a dozen other qualities that girls counted as desirable. He was *short,* mostly—at least short was what he saw when he looked in the mirror.

But as he stepped down the aisle, another voice inside him spoke, reminding him of what he and his friends had accomplished: The remaining kingfishers were safe. Zach Morgan and Eli were under trial and would probably pay a tremendous fine. Congress had closed down the logging in Pine Bluff, and Monarch Lumber was petitioning to log in another area of forest, far from the kingfishers' nesting area.

It wasn't a bad scorecard.

Caitlyn smiled at him as he approached, and she scooted over so Mattie would have a place to sit. "Hi."

"Hi," said Mattie. He sat down.

So here he was, sitting next to Caitlyn Shaughnessy, outside of class, away from homework, away from his friends. For weeks he had wondered what he would say if he ever wound up in this position, and now that he *was* in this position, he had an entirely different thought on his mind: How would he get Latisha Johnson out of here?

Caitlyn held up an empty drink cup. "Latisha," she asked, "would you get me a refill?"

Latisha was sucking the salt off a french fry. The plate in front of her was stacked with wet, droopy, saltless potato sticks. She looked at Caitlyn, then at Mattie, then at Caitlyn again. Then she took the cup and walked off, the french fry dangling from her mouth.

Mattie waited until she was halfway to the soda fountain.

"Listen," he said, "I was wondering—well, I was wondering…" He took a very deep breath. "Well, my friends and I are going to catch a movie at the mall Saturday, and I was wondering if you'd—you know—would like to, I don't know, maybe come with us."

Latisha had already filled the cup and was waiting in a very short line to pay for the drink. She would return shortly, and Mattie had a terrifying sense that the moment was getting away from him.

"Cool," said Caitlyn.

That was it? *Cool?*

"That's a yes?" asked Mattie.

"Sure," said Caitlyn. "I mean, I'll have to ask my mom, but—yeah, sure."

Mattie looked down at the Day Runner sitting on the table. Everything in Caitlyn's life was in that book. Mattie had seen it—phone numbers, addresses, appointments, daily notes to herself like "Bring *Time* magazine to history class" or "Buy .05mm leads for mechanical pencil." Looking at it now, Mattie felt this overwhelming need to be at least as important as the pencil leads. "So," he said, gesturing at the book. "Are you going to pencil me in?"

Latisha was on her way back.

Caitlyn looked at Mattie for few moments without speaking. She then reached for her backpack and began fishing around in the outer pocket. She pulled out a neon blue cylinder with a cap on the end. She tugged off the cap and held the cylinder up so Mattie could see it more closely. It had a ballpoint tip.

She sat a little closer to him as she opened the book to Saturday's date. "For you," she said, "I'll use ink."

C.1